MILES LEDOUX

POP GOES THE WEASEL

Winter in Veil, Book 5

First published by ABCs 2025

This novel is entirely a work of fiction. The names, characters and incidents portrayed in it are the work of the author's imagination. Any resemblance to actual persons, living or dead, events or localities is entirely coincidental.

First edition

ISBN: 978-1-882508-85-3

Cover art by Rachel Kelli
Editing by Julie Mianecki

This book was professionally typeset on Reedsy.
Find out more at reedsy.com

Preface

I went to the grocery store
  I thought a little cheese'll
  Be 'nough to catch a mouse on the floor
  Pop! goes the weasel
  But the mouse was very bright
  He wasn't a mouse to wheedle
  He took the cheese and said, "Goodnight!"
  Pop! goes the weasel

Prologue

"Rob's—dead?"

Deputy Jen Grogan's arm went protectively around the shoulders of her sixteen-year-old daughter, Cyanne. They were in the office of the sheriff of Veil. It was nearly eleven o'clock at night, on a school night. Jen had pointed this out to Sheriff Dubowski when he'd called and said he needed them to come to the station. She'd asked him if this could wait till tomorrow. "No," he'd said gravely—but firmly.

Cy let out a short, humorless laugh. When everyone in the room looked at her, she said, "Sorry, it's just… The last thing I told him was that he'd die alone."

Jen drew an uneasy breath.

"When did that conversation take place?" asked the sheriff.

"Um…the night we brought Violet home with us, after we rescued Megan Toombs."

"What time?"

"I don't know." Cy's eyes had a blank, faraway look. "How did Rob die?" she asked, almost tonelessly.

"Miss Grogan, I need to know what time you talked to Mr. Mulroy."

Though thrown by the use of her surname, Cy started to shrug with disinterest. Jen squeezed her daughter's forearm without taking her eyes off the sheriff. "Answer him."

1

Cy blinked, seemed to come back to herself. "I, I really don't know. I guess it wasn't too long after we got to the house. Maybe around nine? Yeah, it was probably nine—because it was, like, right before I went to bed, and I woke up after midnight and couldn't get back to sleep. And I remember looking at the clock and thinking, *At least I got three hours.*"

"You're sure it was *after* midnight when you woke up?"

Cy glanced at her mother and shrugged at the sheriff. "It was twelve-something."

"Was it raining?" The question came from Deputy Benno, standing beside the sheriff's desk. Flanking the sheriff on his other side was Deputy Derrick, who glared at the younger, most junior deputy for interrupting the sheriff's formal interview.

Cy frowned as she thought back. "Y-yeah, it was."

"That puts it at twelve-forty-five or later—sir."

"Thank you, Deputy." The sheriff leaned toward Cy, interlaced his fingers, and put his next question as delicately as he could. "Why did you tell Rob Mulroy he would die alone?"

Cy seemed to shrink into herself. "He was being a jerk," she mumbled. At the silence that followed she hurried on, "He told me Mom was lying to me about how Dad died, and he said he'd tell me what really happened, but only if I...went out with him again."

The sheriff glanced down and kept his voice mild. "Why didn't you want to go out with him?"

"Keith." Jen had never spoken to Dubowski in that tone before. The look she gave him was both pleading and warning.

With sorrowful eyes, the sheriff said to Cy, "You don't have to answer, and you may request to have an attorney present, but I still have to ask you—"

"He assaulted me," Cy blurted, shaking her head in impatience.

2

"While we were going out, he assaulted me. That's why I broke up with him."

Derrick and Dubowski kept their expressions neutral while Benno quietly smoldered. The sheriff turned to Jen and asked, "You knew about this?"

Jen's hand found Cy's as she replied evenly, "I knew that he'd behaved badly toward her. I didn't know about the assault until shortly before Halloween—*after* Rob had disappeared."

"And where were you on the night of October fifteenth, at midnight?"

"I was asleep at home."

"And today?"

Jen blinked. "Sir?"

"Can you and your daughter account for your whereabouts today?"

Jen's eyes flicked to the other deputies, but predictably they gave nothing away. "The *whole* day?" she asked.

The sheriff said nothing. Cy looked from him to the deputies in confusion. "Why are you asking about today—"

Jen tapped Cy's wrist and said kindly, "No, honey, he can't tell us that."

Still befuddled, her daughter replied, "Well, I was in school…"

"And as you know, I was here," said Jen, "giving Violet a tour of the station so she can start as an intern. Then she shadowed me for part of my patrol…"

"And when I got out of school, I came here and we took Violet to the—"

"*Sheriff.*"

Deputy Benno drew everyone's attention as he stepped to the side of the desk so as to face the sheriff more fully. "Sheriff," he said more calmly, "They didn't do it. You *know* they didn't."

3

Sheriff Dubowski did not look pleased at the insubordination, but at first he said nothing. He gazed thoughtfully from Benno to the interviewees. Just as he began to speak, another voice interrupted him: "He's right, sir."

Jen straightened up in surprise.

"Any evidence we have against the Grogans is circumstantial," said Deputy Derrick. "I think we can eliminate them from further inquiry." He kept his eyes on the sheriff, avoiding Jen's stare of amazement.

The sheriff heaved a long sigh. Then, standing, he said, "Jen Grogan, did you or Cyanne have anything to do with the murder of Rob Mulroy?"

"No, sir, of course not."

"Then I think we've gone enough by the book." Contritely he added, "I'm sorry I put you both through that."

"Wait, I don't understand," said Cy, glancing at all the adults in turn. "It's over, just like that? Aren't we your main suspects?"

Dubowski flashed a smile as Jen threw Cy an exasperated look. "Sweetie," she said through her teeth, "when a law officer says you're off the hook, you don't argue. Now come on." She tugged on Cy's arm as she stood up.

"Actually," said the sheriff, holding up his hand, "next we need to speak to Violet. But before we do, *Deputy* Grogan, I'd like to bring you up to speed. That is, if you're willing to help us with this investigation."

His voice was even, steady, but Jen had known him long enough to recognize the urgency in his eyes. That was the moment she realized this matter went beyond Rob's murder. Something else was going on, something bigger. Dubowski needed her help, but as a courtesy, he was letting her decide for herself.

"Honey," she said to Cy, "I'm gonna give you the house key. Deputy Tan's gonna give you a ride home, and she'll stay with you until Violet and I get back." She didn't add an "Okay?" at the end because it was not a request.

Once Cy was off home, Jen said to the sheriff, "All right, what are we dealing with?"

I

"The girl with no memory of her past possesses a secret that will shake the town of Veil to its core."

Violet listened to Tuck Fleagle's tremulous voice with growing incredulity. She threw a questioning glance at Jen, whose reply was a minuscule shrug. Jen, herself, had only just listened to the recording a few minutes ago.

"It's her destiny to bring down a great evil that's festered here for years. Their showdown is inevitable—" Fleagle's voice broke off suddenly.

"What? What is it?" That was the voice of Rob Mulroy, the young man Violet had prevented from assaulting Cy when they first met. The man who had then disappeared, and who, apparently, was now dead, murdered.

"Someone's here!" shouted Fleagle. "Someone followed us! Followed you!"

"No one followed us!"

All at once Violet's breath caught. They had warned her before playing the recording, so she knew what was coming, but suddenly, as she realized the event was only moments away, she wasn't sure she was ready...

"Let me go! They'll kill me!"

She could tell them to stop the playback if she spoke now...

"Just tell me—"
"Let me go—"
BANG.

Violet inhaled sharply, her eyes shut. Fighting to unclench her teeth, she listened as Rob Mulroy choked out his last breaths. She heard the thud of his body collapsing, felt her skin crawl at the wetness of the sound.

Try as she might to forget, this experience would be burned into her memory forever.

She felt Jen's hand on her shoulder and tried to focus on that.

"I...I don't understand! Why him and not me?" When no answer came, Tuck Fleagle's footsteps took off at a breakneck tempo.

The sheriff stopped the playback and said, "There's forty more minutes of Fleagle running and wheezing and rummaging around. He doesn't say anything more."

Violet swallowed. She pushed her gaze up from the digital recorder to look at Benno. "You haven't found Tuck Fleagle?"

"No," said Benno. "I came across this recording when I searched his apartment. Our working theory is that Mulroy brought the recorder to the interview and turned it on secretly, and then, as he was dying, he slipped it into Fleagle's pocket."

Violet passed a hand over her mouth; her face felt numb. "I think I preferred the old lady who thought I was some girl who disappeared forty years ago. At least she didn't get killed because of me."

A morbid fixation had drawn her eyes back to the digital recorder; therefore she missed the quick look that passed between the sheriff and his deputies.

Dubowski said to her, "One reason we withheld this information from you was that I presumed you wouldn't have any idea what Fleagle was talking about, what with your memory loss."

"Not a clue," Violet confirmed. In her head, with maddening clarity, Rob Mulroy's death replayed over and over. She tried to make it stop and couldn't. Taking a deep breath and resigning herself to the ongoing nightmare, she said, "So who is Tuck Fleagle?"

The sheriff glanced at the others in puzzlement. "Beg pardon?"

"At the radio station, Rod Piper said Fleagle was a morose drunk and an unreliable employee. That's all I know about him. How long has he lived in Veil? Where did he work before the radio station? Who or what is he that might pertain to how he knows me?"

"Violet…" The sheriff pushed aside the recorder so he could fold his hands on the desk. "I understand that, with Fleagle being the first and only clue we've found that could lead us to discovering your identity, you'd want to pursue that line of inquiry. Rest assured, we're doing everything we can to locate him."

Violet gave him a sidelong glance. "It sounds like a 'but' is coming, which doesn't make any sense. My true identity now figures into a *murder* investigation. Why would you not be—"

"We're not sure that Fleagle's connection to you—if any such connection truly exists—is germane to the case."

Violet was so taken aback, she struggled to form coherent words—and failed. Jen hastened to explain, "Tuck Fleagle has a reputation for advancing conspiracy theories and pretending secret involvement in things that put him in or near the center of drama."

Derrick nodded in agreement. "Just now you mentioned that girl who disappeared in the forest and was never found. Fleagle once claimed he knew what really happened to her. He hinted that he'd helped her escape from a plot to assassinate her, that they even had a love affair."

"But he was killed to—I mean, Rob was killed to stop Fleagle from telling him…" Violet trailed off as Fleagle's last words on the recording echoed back to her, the significance of his question suddenly clear—*why not him?* If the killer's goal really had been to prevent the spread of information about Violet's true identity, then why had *only* Rob been eliminated? It might have been possible—if risky—to leave Rob alive and just kill Fleagle, yet *Fleagle alone* had been spared. Why?

The sheriff unwittingly answered her question: "It's possible Mulroy's murder has nothing to do with you at all. We think— or some of us think," he amended, catching sight of Benno's expression, "that his being killed during a discussion about you…was just a coincidence."

There's more to it, Violet realized. There was more they hadn't told her yet. But what? Violet turned to Jen and asked the question with her eyes.

Delicately Jen said, "We think whoever killed Rob…also killed Marcy."

Violet's heartbeat shook her eardrums.

"And Matt Foley, too. And possibly several other people, though I'm not sure I'm sold on that."

Matt Foley, the obnoxious atheist? He was dead?? "I don't understand."

"Violet," said the sheriff, "Deputy Benno tells me that when he hit a dead end investigating the disappearances of Mulroy and Foley, he came to you on Halloween night and you helped him. In *one evening,* you gave him the clues that led him to discover both men had been murdered."

"I did?" Violet remembered Benno had come to her for help

specifically with Mulroy's case, but Foley had only come up in conversation briefly.

"You helped him uncover leads he never would've found otherwise. Did you mention either case to anyone?"

"No." Halloween was the night she'd become friends with college girl–wannabe Marcy Temple, and Marcy had been found murdered the next day. Violet's adventure with Benno had been swiftly forgotten (to put it somewhat inaccurately, in her case).

The sheriff went on, "If I can keep counting on your discretion, I'd like to put what we know before you and see if you spot any patterns, the way you've done before."

She knew he was referring not just to her helping Benno, but to the other mysteries she'd found herself involved in since she'd woken up with no memory of who she was. First there had been the missing eleven-year-old girl, then the witch with the malicious stalker. On Halloween, Veil had been terrorized by a local superstition come to life, and last week, the Grogans' neighbors had been poisoned. In each case, to help uncover the truth, Violet had used her newfound gift: her ability to remember perfectly everything she saw and did, which contrasted so ironically with her *in*ability to recall her own identity.

For a moment, Violet experienced a flash of impostor syndrome. How could she, the most helpless person in Veil, the lost girl without a name or a home, be of any help to anyone? How could she of all people be expected to assist in so serious a matter as a murder investigation? She should tell them to push her out, to go find a more reliable consultant.

She drew an unsteady breath. "I'll try."

Gravely the sheriff drew a tablet from his desk drawer and

activated it. "I need to ask you to look at these photographs," he said.

Violet had a sinister suspicion as to what she would see, but the first image still surprised her. "That's your car," she said ingenuously to Benno, who suddenly looked ill. The next photo explained why: two young men occupied the back seat of the vehicle, both of them in unnatural poses. As the perspective drew nearer in each successive image, the blankness in their eyes and the pallor of their skin grew clearer. Repressing a shudder, Violet strove to maintain a clinical attitude. She observed the bullet wound in Rob Mulroy's chest, the gory dents in Matt Foley's cranium, and the cardboard signs hanging from each of their necks.

"The bodies were discovered a few hours ago," said the sheriff. "We suspect the killer somehow found out that Deputy Benno had taken point in this line of inquiry, and left a message for him to find."

Throwing Benno a sympathetic glance, Violet squinted to read the words on the signs, "W-weasel…" The other word looked like *Monkey*. Instantly a certain nursery rhyme popped— no pun intended—into her head.

"'Pop Goes the Weasel,'" muttered Deputy Derrick. "Each of the three killings ties in to a verse in the song." Adopting the tone of an expert, he added, "Almost every serial killer has a signature."

Violet felt goosebumps rise on the back of her neck. "Serial killer…" Could one really exist here in Veil? This town seemed too small, too quiet for such a horror.

Then part of what Derrick had said finally registered, and she frowned. "Wait, doesn't 'Pop Goes the Weasel' only have one verse?"

"Apparently it has ten or more," said Jen. "Wish I'd known that when I was raising my kids. Drove me crazy, singing the same verse over and over." She reached toward a cabinet, took a pair of pages stapled together and placed it before Violet. It was a copy of the full lyrics of "Pop Goes the Weasel." Violet was struck immediately by the first line: *All around the cobbler's bench.* Shouldn't it be, *All around the mulberry bush?* She was aware of another nursery rhyme that began with, *Here we go 'round the mulberry bush.* Perhaps, over time, confusion had caused the lyrics of one song to bleed into the other.

Still affecting an air of expertise (and drawing an annoyed glare from Benno), Derrick went on, "Mulroy was apparently the 'weasel,' and the 'pop' was the gunshot that killed him. The coroner estimates Foley was killed about three weeks ago; we already knew he'd been attacked on the Greene River footbridge and knocked into the water with a stick." He pointed at the first part of the eighth verse on the page:

Ev'ry night when I go out
  The monkey's on the table
  Take a stick and knock it off
  Pop! goes the weasel

Someone had drawn an arrow from those lyrics to a scribbled word, *Foley*. Another arrow matched the next set of lines to the name, *Temple*. Violet's breath caught...

Put some pepper on his nose
  And you'll make him sneeze-l
  Catch him fast before he snaps
  Pop! goes the weasel

12

Violet looked up, suddenly seething with outrage and horror. "You're saying someone snapped poor Marcy's neck because of one word in a stupid song?!"

As gently as possible, Benno remarked, "The killer also sprinkled pepper on her nose post-mortem. That's what first drew our attention to the connection to this nursery rhyme."

Violet shook her head and brushed away a tear. "Why did it have to be her?" When Jen gave her a commiserating look, she said, "No, I'm serious. Why kill these people in particular? How does he choose his victims?"

"That, we're not sure of," said the sheriff.

Hesitantly, Benno said, "Well…"

The sheriff nodded. "Go ahead."

Benno picked up a sheaf of notes from the windowsill. "There have been several other unexplained deaths over the past few years in this region that *might* be the work of the same killer. Each case has a slight connection to 'Pop Goes the Weasel.'"

"*Very* slight," Jen commented.

Undeterred, Benno went on, "Here's a case in Stowe where two people died from food poisoning, a…" He shuffled through the papers. "A Vicky Rushton and a Bert Cash. If you look at the first verse…" He pointed at the lyrics. Violet read through the familiar lines about the monkey chasing the weasel and thinking it was "all in fun." Next she expected to see the lines that tended to follow, involving pennies, a thread, and a needle. Instead she found a set of lyrics she'd never seen or heard before:

Queen Victoria's very sick
*   Prince Albert has the measles*
*   The children have the whooping cough*
*   Pop! goes the weasel*

"It could be," Benno surmised, "those two were chosen because of their names. Another pair of victims were father and son, which could refer to the fourth verse. Another victim was a painter—"

"But," interrupted Violet, "if he's following the song, then why choose Marcy when the line says, 'Put some pepper on *his* nose? Catch *him* fast before *he* snaps?'"

Benno was at a loss.

Violet felt her eyes burning with tears, her jaw quivering, as she read through the lyrics. What sort of person would think of this children's song and be inspired to commit murder?

Jen saw the sudden twitch in Violet's chin, the sudden focus in her eyes. She knew, before Violet even said anything, that she'd recalled something important. In a moment, Violet would unveil a breathtaking revelation.

Violet inhaled and began to whistle. She started with just a few notes, then paused and started again, in a different key.

Unsettled, Derrick demanded, "What are you—" but Jen silenced him with a sharp gesture.

Violet made it all the way to the high note, the "Pop!" Then she stopped.

Jen made a guess: "You remember someone whistling that song?"

Violet nodded slowly, her eyes still far away.

"Who?" Benno asked quickly.

Violet's face slowly creased with strain. "I...can't..." She shut her eyes, bared her teeth. "I don't think I saw who it was. I just heard them."

"Where?" asked the sheriff. "When?"

Violet opened her eyes and shook her head in amazement and despair. "I don't remember!"

14

Her listeners were dumbfounded by this statement. Derrick snorted. "I thought you had a perfect memory."

"Derrick," the sheriff said quietly, warningly.

Violet couldn't understand what was happening. There were times when she'd had difficulty finding the right trigger to bring to light a particular sought-after memory, but once the memory had been located she *never* had trouble recalling all its details. Not unless she had been less than fully conscious at the time the memory had been formed, but she was almost sure that wasn't the case here. Having recalled the incident, the memories should be all but forcing themselves on her, as they always did. Now, at a moment when recalling those details was crucial, why were they not forthcoming?!

Violet took a deep breath and strove to filter out the sounds of the present, the fidgeting of the people around her. Sometimes her memories felt so real that she mistook them for the present. If she tried to believe that about the whistling, maybe she could bring herself back to that moment…

The musical notes played in her head. They were coming from behind her, which confirmed she hadn't seen the whistler. But what *could* she see? Nothing came to her. Was it dark? Were her eyes closed? No…no, she could sense that she possessed the ability to see, but for some reason she just *wouldn't*. It was almost as if, in her mind, she was looking away from the vision.

As strange as this thought was, it occurred to Violet: even if she was looking away, might she be able to spot some small detail out of the metaphorical corner of her eye?

All at once Violet snatched a pad of paper and a pen off the desk. The others watched as she made a quick sketch.

"Is…that a leaf?" asked Benno.

Violet shrugged as she leaned back in her chair, relieved the image hadn't faded before she'd finished the drawing. "It's the only thing I can picture in connection with the whistling."

Jen turned the pad to get a closer look at the image. "You're saying you saw this at the same time you heard the song?"

"I think so."

Derrick looked at her askance. "You saw a leaf?"

Violet shook her head. "No, it wasn't a leaf. It was an outline, a *picture* of a leaf."

"Was it colored in?" asked Jen.

"No."

Dubowski traced the points of the leaf with his finger. "From the shape, it looks like red oak."

Benno craned his neck. "Was it straight up and down like that when you saw it?"

In truth, Violet wasn't sure, but she nodded.

"Could be a graphic symbol," suggested Jen. "Company logo?"

"Pressler's corporation has a leaf as its symbol," Derrick jumped to point out.

"No," said the sheriff, "that's a striped maple."

They photographed Violet's sketch and searched for the image online, but it returned no matches. Violet tried and tried to make herself remember more, but nothing came to her. It seemed they'd reached an impasse.

It was past midnight by the time they all departed the station. Benno volunteered to stay and continue to scour the internet, as he wouldn't be getting any sleep that night anyway.

Sheriff Dubowski intended to leave along with the others, but he was held up by Deputy Hayden. "We have a problem," she told him hesitantly.

"Unless it's another dead body, it can wait till tomorrow," he said, yawning.

"Sir, dispatch got a call about an audio file that just appeared on the Veil community website. I tried to get through to the administrator to get it taken down, but it's already been downloaded. It's gone viral."

"What are you talking about? What audio file?"

Hayden held out her phone and tapped the screen. *"Seriously? You walked here?"*

At first Dubowski showed no reaction.

"I've lived in Veil all my life. I know all the backyard alleys and shortcuts—"

Dubowski jabbed the screen to silence the voices of Mulroy and Fleagle. He took slow, heavy breaths. "How did this get out?" he growled.

Hayden mumbled that she didn't know.

"Find out who leaked this," the sheriff ordered, mostly to get her out of his hair. This was going to be a long night.

The plan had been to inform the public about the serial killer via a carefully planned report. Now, everyone in town would know by morning.

The sheriff's department was about to face widespread panic.

II

FIVE DAYS LATER

Trisha Sinclair jolted awake as the bus jostled itself into forward motion. Her neck was cramped from sleeping in an awkward position. She winced, stretched, and glanced out the window. Nearby road signs told her the bus had just made its first stop after crossing into Vermont. Somewhere in New Hampshire the passing wintry landscape had put her to sleep. The Green Mountain State, however, seemed to be thawing; the farther they drove, the less white she saw on the ground.

Only one other passenger occupied the bus, sitting farther up front. Trisha wasn't surprised. Thanksgiving week wasn't yet close enough to bring heavy amounts of travel. She, herself, would've been among the forthcoming mob of home-goers had it not been for the snowstorm that canceled all class days between now and the holidays, affording her a chance to spend some extra time with relatives she rarely saw anymore. Trisha wasn't happy about falling behind in her courses, but as far as public transportation went, she preferred it like this: quiet, less crowded, serene. Much like her destination.

She wondered how Veil would look when she reached it.

Would half the town still have their Halloween decorations up? Was it still warm enough for clusters of children to be out and about on bicycles and scooters? Last time they'd spoken via computer screen, Great Aunt Althea had mentioned heavy snowfall, but the fluctuating temperatures had probably melted it.

A crease formed between Trisha's brows at the thought of her aunt. Althea had sworn to Trisha in her last email that she and Delphine were fine, but Trisha was anxious to see for herself. What sort of heartless bastard would break into their house and terrorize two of the world's sweetest old ladies? Apparently the home invasion had been part of some larger, more convoluted criminal plot, but Trisha didn't care—as long as whoever had done it was locked up and unable to cause further harm. Althea had ordered her not to worry herself, but Trisha couldn't help it. She wouldn't be who she was today without her two aunts (Delphine wasn't technically an aunt, but she was close enough). Trisha would only feel at ease once she saw for herself that they were all right. She was so worried she'd almost called…him…to ask if he would look in on them for her.

Almost.

Before Trisha fully realized it, the bus was passing through Platte and entering Veil's outskirts. She must have been quite lost in her own head for her not to notice.

Then she frowned, pressing her face closer to the glass.

This couldn't be Veil, she thought absurdly. This had to be a life-size replica. Sure, all the buildings were where they were supposed to be, all the street names were the same, and there was no mistaking the mountain range on one side, but there the resemblance ended. Even when bad weather forced its people indoors and the streets had little traffic, Veil still had a particular kind of energy Trisha had always felt but never been able to describe. It was an energy that drew her, excited her, made her curious and adventuresome. At one point in her life, it had even made her decide—briefly—to call this town her home.

Now there seemed to be almost no energy at all—wait...

There *was* something. Something that went beyond the dearth of activity that made Veil look like a ghost town. As she observed the patrol cars parked seemingly around every corner, the "closed" signs on most of the small businesses—on a *Monday*—and the odd face here and there peeking out from behind upstairs window curtains, Trisha knew...

Something was happening in Veil. Something wrong. Something frightening.

Trisha's theory was all but confirmed when she passed by the school. Adjacent to the slanted row of school buses was an area designated for student pickup by parents or guardians. Today this side-lot was gridlocked as far more vehicles than it was designed to accommodate tried to get in and out. Horns honked and blared. Some harried teachers attempted to alleviate the problem by guiding traffic and helping students locate their rides more quickly. Not a single student was leaving on foot.

The adults are afraid of letting kids walk home alone, Trisha realized.

Her bus pulled up to the station just off Main Street. Trisha moved into the aisle and stretched her legs. Althea and Delphine lived only two streets away; she could lug her suitcase that far. Her fellow passenger apparently had no luggage, for he was already disembarking—

Trisha drew a sharp gasp. The man had been sitting so far ahead of her, she only ever saw the top of his head. She hadn't known...

20

Instantly she was equal parts torn between going after him and ducking down so he wouldn't see her. What could she possibly say to him? She'd considered the possibility of what to do if she ran into him during this trip, but worry over her aunts had overshadowed that concern (or, more likely, had provided her with an excuse to avoid thinking about it). Seeing him now, she felt she *had* to at least greet him…didn't she? If only she could come up with a coherent sentence or two to say to him—but the English language had suddenly deserted her.

For he had just seen her. He'd caught sight of her through the bus windows as he walked alongside. He'd frozen mid-stride, his mouth open.

Trisha swallowed. Waved shakily.

Benno managed to give her one stiff nod before he strode away, trying overly hard to hurry without anyone perceiving his haste.

Trisha nearly dropped back into her seat, her mortification drowning out the part of her asking herself what Benno had been doing, taking the bus. At least now she no longer needed to wonder what would happen if she bumped into her former fiancé.

"Welcome to Veil," said the driver as, a minute later, she tipped him and stepped off the bus.

Trisha had a fleeting, irrational thought that she should turn around, plant herself back in her seat and not for any reason whatsoever set foot in this town, that something terrible would happen to her if she stayed. She put the feeling down to her encounter with Benno just now and ignored the impulse.

* * *

"Good evening, Veil. This is Rod Piper at KVLM with the seven-o'clock local news.

21

"*The town-hall debate between mayoral candidates Elijah Pressler and Kurt Riner will take place tomorrow at four in the afternoon at the Veil Community Center. In order to ensure the debate begins in a timely manner, attendees are asked to arrive at least fifteen minutes early.*

"*A friendly reminder that the sheriff department's nine-o'clock curfew is still in effect. Anyone out-of-doors between the hours of 9 p.m. and 6 a.m. without authorization will be in violation of this directive.*

"*As a matter of fact, I have Sheriff Dubowski in the studio with me at this moment. He has a request he'd like to make directly. Go ahead, Sheriff.*"

"*Thank you, Rod. Good evening. Before I say what I'm about to say, I'd just like to mention that I've run it by both mayoral candidates, and each of them gave it their proverbial seal of approval. Its purpose is not to advance anyone's political agenda, but simply public safety. So, here goes.*

"*I know everyone is frightened. I know businesses have started closing early, and in some cases closing altogether. Some of you haven't left your homes in days. Some of our friends have even left town. With regard to your own safety and the safety of your families, whatever you choose to do is your business. My deputies and I are working round the clock to identify and apprehend the killer, so that everyone can breathe easier and life can go back to normal here.*

"*Until that happens, what I need from you is this: remember that we are still a community. Yes, one individual in Veil might be a murderer. But that does not excuse some of the behavior that's come to my attention. Some of you are treating this situation as a game. If you have a valid reason for suspecting someone, the appropriate thing to do—and the smartest—is to call my department and we will investigate it. What is not appropriate is starting rumors, casting suspicion on people behind their backs, or—and I'm particularly unhappy about this—placing a bet that so-and-so is the killer. My department does not consider 'strong odds' to be evidence. In other words, this is not a game of Mafia. You do not get to vote for who you think is the killer. That is libelous and could incite violence, whether through panic or vigilanteism. No, my department has not shared all the details of the investigation, but you can trust us to relate any information that would increase your safety. If we haven't told you something, then it's not something that would protect you.*

"That's basically all I have to say—except, please...don't speculate on which of my deputies are most likely to get killed off or survive if and when we go to apprehend the murderer. Or if you do, be better at keeping it to yourselves."

"Thank you, Sheriff. That was Keith Dubowski, our local sheriff. Now, Mary DePalma with the weather."

* * *

The question of the killer's identity was one that everyone in Veil was talking about. But there was a deeper question on everyone's minds, which no one spoke of at all.

Next door to the Grogans, the Dosley family went swiftly through the motions of what had, in the last few days, become their nightly routine. They made sure all the doors were locked. They placed jars of marbles and other such items that would make noise just inside each window, so that if any were opened or broken, the intruder would upset the item and make his presence known. They hugged each other tight, and then one of them drank a mug of coffee and sat down in the living room, keeping watch for the first few hours of the night with a baseball bat at hand.

In the village, before going to bed, Rabbi Isaac Metz made sure that every appliance was turned off, so that if anyone entered, he could count on his sensitive hearing and habit of light sleeping to render him instantly awake. What he might do next in that event, he wasn't sure; he hoped that, if and when the moment came, he would know.

In her apartment, Bethany Williams had made an agreement with her roommate to alternate watches throughout the night, but tonight her roommate was apparently staying over at her boyfriend's. All Bethany could think of to do was to pray herself to sleep.

Mayoral candidate Kurt Riner wanted to go to bed, but his fiancée, Amy, insisted he stay up later to prepare for the debate tomorrow. Kurt was confident everything would go as planned, and that the best preparation at this point would be a good night's rest. Amy couldn't understand how he could be so eager to sleep, and asked him if he was feeling well. Kurt said he was feeling fine, and promised her nothing bad would happen to either of them tonight.

Kurt's opponent, Pressler, was also still awake, struggling to think through an ongoing problem, but it had nothing to do with tomorrow's debate. Perhaps the problem would end up taking care of itself, he mused. Perhaps he needn't do anything at all.

And Sheriff Dubowski vigilantly coordinated the patrol of Veil by his deputies, feeling the ache of having slept so little in the past week. He knew he couldn't prevent whatever tragedy was coming next, but if there was any hope for a miracle, any chance he or one of the deputies might happen to be in the right place at the right time, he had to try.

For all these people knew that, one day soon, one of them would be found dead. It might be tonight or another night, but they knew—not all of them would survive.

III

"Looks different without all the ghosts and spiders," Cy remarked.

Violet silently agreed. The interior of the community center was barely recognizable. The only other time she'd seen it was Halloween night. In her mind's eye she could picture the former setup perfectly: the booths, the decorations, the costumed townsfolk, the pumpkin-carving station, the stage for the costume contest, the corner where they'd had the mini–haunted house. She could summon it all to memory perfectly—so why, she wondered for the hundredth time, couldn't she do the same with the serial killer? Why couldn't she remember when and where she'd heard someone whistling "Pop Goes the Weasel"?

Hundreds of chairs had been arranged in curving rows facing a dais with a chair at either end, each with its own microphone. Violet couldn't help but notice how quiet all the Veil citizens were as they filed in: so many people, yet so little noise. Not a subdued silence, as at a funeral, but a tense silence, fraught with anxiety and dread. It had been almost a week since the recording of Mulroy's murder had been leaked, since Sheriff Dubowski had broken the news that there was a serial killer in Veil, who had already claimed at least three victims. Who would be next? Those who hadn't fled the town dreaded to find out, and had all but barricaded themselves in their homes. According to Cy, it was only thanks to a massive email campaign spearheaded by both mayoral candidates that this many people had turned out here today. More sheriff's deputies than Violet had ever seen in one place were stationed all around the room.

"Oh, come on!"

Heads turned at the sudden break in the silence. It had come from the entranceway.

"Oh no," Jen murmured from where she stood next to Cy and Violet, having just escorted them in. She hurried back toward the door, where two deputies were struggling with a shabbily-dressed woman about Jen's age.

"Come on, it was in a sheath!" the woman protested. "It wasn't technically concealed!"

"Ma'am," grunted a burly deputy, "you can't bring weapons in here, concealed or not." With one last tug he pried the ten-inch knife from her fingers.

"Oh, sure!" the woman drawled. "Like half the people in this room aren't armed!"

Jen hurried up to the woman's side. "Myrna—"

"Why don't you search the rest of the people here, huh?"

"Myrna, come sit by me, okay?" Jen led her away.

"It wasn't even one of my big ones!" Myrna could be heard complaining.

"No way," Cy breathed. Violet looked over to see her march up to another woman in the crowd, who had been watching the scene and jotting something on a notepad.

The scene with Myrna had broken some of the tension in the room. Scattered murmurs and whispers came from all corners, so it didn't draw much attention when Cy said rather confrontationally, "Excuse me, Ms. Upshaw."

Kelly Upshaw, the *Veil Chronicle* reporter, looked up and regarded Cy with thinly concealed chagrin. "Yes?"

"You're not planning on writing anything scathing or embarrassing in the paper about Myrna Redpath, are you?"

Kelly moved her eyes upward, as if to roll them, then seemed to gather her patience and said crisply, "Journalism is about reporting facts. How they reflect on people isn't our concern."

"Oh," said Cy, adopting a falsely ingenuous tone. "So you'd write anything newsworthy about Myrna, whether it put her in a bad light or good?"

"Exactly."

"Then why didn't your paper say anything about how she saved my life a few weeks ago?" When Kelly didn't have a ready answer, Cy pressed on, "It mentioned everyone else who was there, but left her out."

Kelly seemed to be considering her response, then evidently decided it wasn't worth the effort and instead answered, "If you think we could improve how we do our reporting, you're free to write a letter to the editor."

"I'll be sure to do that," said Cy. "And I'll be sure to mention your article about the Wiccan sabbat last month."

Violet had been scanning for a pair of seats where she and Cy could sit together, but this last remark sharply riveted her attention.

"What about it?" Kelly almost snapped.

"Oh, I don't know, maybe the fact that in an article about Wiccans, you quoted literally *every* person at the sabbat who was *not* Wiccan! I mean, no wonder Candy's fighting for representation—"

"One of those people I quoted was you."

"Oh, I remember," said Cy. "I remember because you *mis*quoted me."

Kelly's arms went down to her sides. She was nearing the end of her patience. "I have never misquoted anyone in my life."

Violet could picture Kelly's article in her head, word for word, even as Cy replied, "Every time I used the word 'witch,' you replaced it with 'Pagan' in brackets."

"That's not a misquote. If we believe it will improve reader clarity, we're allowed to—"

"You're not worried about clarity, you're worried about having the word 'witch' in your paper—because it's a taboo! A taboo based on discrimination and fear!"

Kelly lowered her voice slightly. "If we use the term, 'witches,' people might start to think there are actual witches in Veil!"

"There *are* actual witches!"

"Not as far as the people of Veil are concerned. Their definition of the term is different from—"

"Then people are wrong!"

"It's not our job to tell people they're wrong."

"It kind of *is!*"

Kelly pocketed her notepad. "I'm tired of this conversation. For the record, you're the only one who's complained about that article." As she said this, both she and Cy directed a glance at Violet, as if expecting her to add her voice to Cy's.

Violet had possibly been about to do precisely that, but at that moment she felt her tongue stick in her throat, her thoughts suddenly foggy and sluggish. She felt her cheeks burn, knowing she looked like a deer in headlights.

When it became obvious Violet had nothing to contribute, Kelly stalked off, ignoring Cy's parting shot: "If Candy were still around, you can bet she'd be all up in arms about it!" She continued to mutter to herself as they made their way to their seats. "You know what I'm gonna do? I'm gonna major in journalism so I can join the *Chronicle* and replace jerks like her."

"That's good," Violet replied tonelessly.

Cy's mood softened immediately. "I'm sorry. I shouldn't have brought up Candy. I know it probably still hurts to think about her."

Violet forced a smile. "It's fine."

Cy laid a hand on her back. "You haven't heard from her at all?"

Violet shook her head tensely. "That's not why I'm upset. I was right there with you. I should've spoken up for her, same as you. I just stood there like a dummy."

"Well…" Cy half-shrugged. "Confrontation's more *my* thing. Your thing's being smart."

"Not lately." Violet fell into a sulk as the deputy mayor asked everyone to finish taking their seats so the debate could begin.

* * *

"Benno?"

Deputy Benno looked up in genuine surprise. The past twenty-four hours, he'd struggled to keep his focus on the investigation while part of him debated whether to pay a call to the former love of his life. He'd told himself time and again that she wouldn't want to see him, and now here she was, dropping in on *him*.

The slender girl with short, curly, dark hair gave him an awkward, jerky wave. "Hi."

"Hi," he echoed, staring at her.

Trisha looked all around, everywhere but his eyes. "Looks like you've got the station all to yourself."

Benno looked about and was almost startled to find himself in the empty sheriff's station. He was seated at one of the work terminals in the conference room. "Everybody else just headed to the debate," he explained as the English language came back to him.

"Debate?"

"The election for mayor is coming up. They've having a town hall debate today."

"Oh, right, of course. Delphine and Althea mentioned that."

Benno swallowed. He'd been brooding on this since last night. He knew what he had to ask. "Trisha—"

"So I was surprised to see you on the bus yesterday," she cut him off, unintentionally.

"I, um, had to interview someone in Keene for a case. Had to do it in person. And my car's...not currently usable."

When he didn't elaborate further, Trisha drew a quick breath and abruptly changed the subject. "I'm visiting Aunt Althea and Delphine."

"Yeah, you just said."

"Right." She winced. "I just wanted to thank you for looking out for them."

At that, Benno smiled, and he managed to relax a little. "They're the ones who look out for me," he told her. "The first few months here in Veil, I didn't know anyone, didn't know how to go about building a home and a personal life. Your aunts—well, you know them, they're incredibly kind. They helped me feel not alone."

Though she was trying to smile, Benno saw the tears glistening in Trisha's eyes just before she looked down. Quickly, he moved toward her. "I wasn't trying to make you feel bad," he assured her.

She nodded, not looking at him. "It is kind of my fault, though," she said thickly.

Benno resisted the urge to take her in his arms. "How's your new major going?" he asked.

Trisha looked at him blankly for a moment, as if bewildered by the question. "It's going…really hard, actually. It's a whole new way of thinking for me, of looking at human behavior. A whole different set of tools for education." She looked him in the eye. "It's made me more sure than ever that I made the right decision."

"Trish, I know you did—"

"I know you're still angry at me, and I still regret hurting you, but I stand by what I—"

"Trish." Gently Benno grasped her wrist. "I'm not angry. If there's anyone who should be angry, it's you." When she gave him a look of bemusement, he went on, "I was never upset because I thought your decision was wrong. I was angry at myself—I knew I ought to have been more supportive. I knew you were hurting, too, but I shut you out anyway."

Trisha shook her head. "You had every right to…"

"You were making the hardest decision of your life, and I wasn't there for you. I expected you to just put my needs first. That's not what partners do." He took her hand in both of his. "Can you forgive me?"

Trisha brushed away a tear, then placed her other hand on top of his. "If you can forgive me."

Benno flashed a smile. "Deal."

Trisha let out a soft breath, relief smoothing out the lines of tension on her face. "Thank you," she mouthed. Then, swallowing, she said, "I've missed you."

Benno nodded. Both of them gave a quiet, comfortable laugh.

Together they looked down at their hands, still clasped.

Trisha looked into his eyes, then down again, and he understood. She was leaving the decision up to him. She would consent either way.

Gently, he let her go.

After a moment, Trisha said, "I'd probably better go meet my aunts. I figure the debate hasn't hired an ASL interpreter."

"Probably not," Benno agreed.

Trisha half-turned to leave, then, squeezing her hands together as if for courage, she turned back. "Do you wanna come over for dinner tonight? With me and my aunts?"

Benno tipped his chin down, grinning.

Trisha leaned her head back in realization. "They already asked you. I guess I'll see you later then." She shook her head in amused disapproval.

"Trisha, wait." The use of her full name got her attention. "Did they tell you about the serial killer?"

She nodded and touched his arm. "I'll be careful, I promise." Leaning in, she gave him a quick kiss on the cheek. "See ya."

Benno sat back down at his work station, awash with emotion over the unexpected closure. He'd long ago given up hope.

"Oh!"

Benno looked up to see that Trisha had stopped again, near the door.

"Haven't seen that for a long time," she remarked. Then she left.

Benno glanced over to see what she was talking about. On the wall hung a copy of the leaf design Violet had drawn from memory, which thus far no one had been able to identify.

He bolted after Trisha, knocking over his chair.

32

IV

"The next question," boomed the basso profundo voice of Rod Piper, "is... 'Both of you served on Veil's school board, and both of you have made what were, at the time, considered controversial choices. If faced with them again, would you make those same decisions now? Mr. Riner, we'll start with you."

Trisha was right: no one had hired an ASL interpreter for this event, and it irked her. Althea had remarked that Benno sometimes volunteered as a translator around Veil; it was a shame he couldn't be here. He'd seemed very perturbed when Trisha explained to him where she'd seen the leaf symbol hanging on the wall. She wondered why it was important.

"Well," said Riner from where he sat on the right side of the dais, "I guess it depends on whether you want the short answer or the longer version—"

"Why not both?" Pressler asked from the opposite side of the dais. Throughout the debate so far, they'd maintained an informal framework wherein the candidates had interrupted each other once or twice—mostly to deliver quips and one-liners like this last. Trisha had to assume they'd made an agreement with those who were in charge of the debate that they wouldn't let these interruptions get too disruptive.

"Sure," Riner replied casually, "I can give you both. Uh, short answer: yes. I would of course make the same decision I did back then; it wasn't a difficult choice. But then..." He paused, seemingly staring into space. Trisha held her hands in midair, waiting for him to finish his sentence. Her arms were starting to ache; Delphine would take over translating for Althea in a few minutes.

"But then," Riner repeated, "my decision, itself, wasn't the source of the controversy, and that's where the...the longer version comes in. The question of whether or not to impose a stricter dress code on the high school ceased to be the central question when..." He stopped again and swallowed.

At first, Trisha was irritated at his stopping and starting, but then she looked at his face more closely: he was grimacing—but also trying not to, as one does when one is in pain and attempting to hide it. Some murmuring behind her told her she wasn't the only one who'd noticed.

"Ceased to be the...central question when the proposed dress code was...altered...to include..."

"Kurt!" A blond woman rushed onto the dais as Riner screwed up his face and doubled over, drawing gasps and cries from the audience. He collapsed onto his knees beside the chair. The sheriff and the blond woman tried to help him to his feet. He gave a sharp groan; any slight movement seemed to pain him.

The next few minutes saw several people clustered about Riner: the deputy mayor, the sheriff, several deputies, and the blond woman (who, Althea informed Trisha, was Riner's fiancée). Rod Piper continually asked the audience to remain calm and in their seats. The only person who seemed at ease was Elijah Pressler, who looked on from where he stood at the opposite end of the dais with something like intrigue.

Eventually Riner was taken outside where he could be loaded into an approaching ambulance.

Rod Piper said into his microphone, "I'm sorry, everyone. It looks like we're going to have to cut the debate short. It's not clear what's wrong with Mr. Riner. He's being taken to the hospital, and if you tune in to KVLM, I'll keep you apprised of his condition. So, thank you all for coming and—"

"Excuse me!" A man in the front row had stood up with his hand raised, one finger pointed upward. He was fortyish, wearing glasses. "I'd like to hear Mr. Pressler's response to that last question. That is, if he's up to it." A murmur spread throughout the crowd, stirred by the overt challenge.

Trisha whispered to Delphine, asking who that was. Delphine said his name was Greg Toombs.

Pressler shrugged nonchalantly and sat down. "I don't mind answering, if it's all right with the moderator."

Rod Piper looked across the room at the deputy mayor, who gave him a resigned nod. "Mr. Riner was given the standard two minutes for a response," he told Pressler. "Since the debate is technically over, restrictions are no longer in effect, but we ask that you contain your answer to the same time limit."

"Of course."

Althea pointed at Pressler and Toombs and signed, *Those two had a fistfight last month.*

It wasn't a fistfight, signed Delphine. *Toombs kicked Pressler in the nuts. That was all.*

Yes, but I wasn't going to say that in polite company, Althea signed back irritably. Trisha fought not to laugh.

"The 'controversial choice,' in my case, was that I voted to cut music theory from the required courses in junior high school. In case you don't know, music 'theory' is where they teach, basically, how to read music—something they teach students anyway if those students join chorus, band, or orchestra. In other words, any student *who actually has an interest in music* would receive the education necessary to pursue that interest. Requiring *all* students to take those courses puts an unnecessary increase on their workload. I saw this as detrimental to the students' well-being, so I helped put a stop to it. I'm proud to be able to look back on it as one of the few times I managed to make a positive difference."

Trisha was so dumbfounded, she'd forgotten to keep translating. She couldn't believe her ears. To hear this man so blithely defend—no, that wasn't the right word—*brag* about what he'd done left her aghast.

Apparently it had had the same effect on Greg Toombs. "There were a lot of people who didn't approve of that decision," he said with thinly veiled fury. "In fact, they were outraged."

Pressler held up his hand in a cease-fire gesture. "I understand," he said gravely, in a tone that made Trisha believe he didn't. "There are always going to be traditionalists who want to keep things the same, even if it's not practical."

That's not what it's about! Trisha wanted to stand up and shout, but nerves restrained her.

"That's why there was such a hue and cry when cursive writing got taken out of school curricula. But think about it—what do we really need cursive for anymore? One day soon, we won't even need *handwriting* anymore. That's a reality of developing technology. It makes some of the old fogeys tremble, but if they make just a little effort to adapt, they'll see it's all right. Maybe in their day, you needed to be able to read music to know how a song goes, but today you can just go on the internet and listen to a recording."

Delphine pointed from Pressler to Toombs and signed, *He's trying to provoke a reaction.*

If so, it was having the desired effect. "Are you on crack??!"

"Greg." The soft but stern warning came from the sheriff.

Rising to his feet, Pressler went on, "Education has an ongoing problem of students not getting to learn enough practical knowledge, and completely useless knowledge is taught in its place." This statement was met with scattered applause.

Toombs threw up his hands. "Who's to say which knowledge is useful or not? When did we stop wanting our kids to have a well-rounded education? You could arbitrarily say *any* school subject is useless. Most kids would say *all* of them are. Are we gonna cut biology for whoever doesn't already want to be a doctor—even though it still applies to their own bodies? Or gym class for those who aren't in sports? If you were really avid about cutting things that have no educational value, you could cut from the sports department, but—" At this, there were several *boos*. "Exactly!" Toombs said in response. "No one wants to do that because sports programs bring in money and acclaims for the school. They're not about education, they're about showing off—"

"No," Pressler snapped, completely ignoring Rod Piper, who was waving at him and pointing to his wristwatch. "No, showing off is teaching kids fancy writing, whose only purpose ever was to help a previous generation pretend they were in a class above others." More applause. "Education shouldn't just be for the elite and the privileged, but for everyone."

Toombs was evidently becoming too angry to remain cogent. "That doesn't even mean anything!" He took deep breaths, trying to rein himself in. "Music theory is not 'elite.' It's basic, like state capitals. Even if the kids aren't going to go into music as a career, what's the big deal? Kids used to learn all sorts of things a few decades ago. Why is it a problem now?"

Pressler eyed him critically. "Are you saying kids today are stupid?"

This brought many disparaging voices directed toward Toombs, who became frantic. "No, I didn't say that!"

Pressler appeared to consider Toombs's question seriously. "Well, who knows?" he said. "Maybe parents back then assumed kids were just being lazy when they got burned out from overwork. Whatever the case, today's parents want things different. I spoke with them, myself, when I was on the school board, and they told me so."

"You can't just treat it like a business! A business with customers and—"

"You're saying the school board should ignore what parents want? What their kids need?"

"Stop putting words in my—"

"Is that what I should do as mayor, ignore what my constituents tell me?"

By now, Toombs was sapped of his ability to form coherent sentences. Red in the face, he looked ready to rush onstage and tackle Pressler—which is no doubt why the sheriff materialized at the man's side and laid a hand on his arm.

Pressler made an expansive gesture, then turned his back to the crowd, shaking his head. Trisha was sure he was hiding a triumphant grin.

"Who knows?" said a voice.

Pressler turned back around, his expression neutral.

His sweaty hands slipped a little on the handle of the microphone.

Trisha craned her neck to see who'd spoken, as did several

other spectators. It was a woman about her age, with dark hair that had a purple streak on one side.

"Sorry, didn't catch that," Pressler replied evenly. The subtext of his demeanor seemed to be, *Sure, I'm ready to face another challenger.*

The woman rose to her feet, her eyes fixed on Pressler. She was very short. She said, "You were talking about why students are having difficulty learning, and you said, 'Who knows?'"

Trisha glanced at Delphine and Althea, who both excitedly signed, *Violet.*

"I don't think that's exactly what I—"

"But you're also acting like you *do* know. Which brings up the question: *how* do you know? Like, how do you know teaching cursive is bad for students?"

Pressler chuckled and gave her a sideways look. "I'm pretty sure you won't find anyone anywhere who would rather have to learn an entirely separate, completely unnecessary iteration of the alphabet. The only people who want it back are those who want today's kids to feel the same torture they were forced to endure, which is pretty selfish of them."

"Maybe *you* don't have any use for it, but couldn't there be people who do?"

"You're saying we should add to the workload of every schoolchild because of the personal preferences of a few?"

Trisha was beginning to recognize the pattern of Pressler's attacks, and she was gratified when Violet didn't rise to the bait. "What if overworked kids are not the result of how *much* they're taught, but *how* they're taught?"

Trisha could've kissed her.

"Well—" Pressler tried to hide the fact that he'd been caught off-guard—"I'm not an expert on the subject—"

"Well, maybe you ought to consult a few of them before you make a big decision—that affects a lot of kids—based on your own assumptions. Did you ask any behavior scientists or education specialists?"

Trisha very nearly waved, thinking, *Right here! Right here!* while in the back of her head she reminded herself, *You're still only a student.*

Pressler was beginning to look peeved. He no longer put on a front of aloof amusement. "So you think cursive should still be taught in school as a requirement."

"Possibly. Maybe not taught as a 'fancy' version of the alphabet, but as a method of writing where you don't have to pick up your pencil between each letter. It might make it easier for students to take notes. After all, it doesn't have to be legible to anyone but themselves. It could help them do better in school."

"You don't know that."

"Correct," Violet answered promptly. "I don't know for the same reason *you* don't know. Neither of us has consulted an expert. But at least one of us has the sense not to assume she knows it already." She looked mildly surprised when this was met with a smattering of applause.

Pressler could obviously see he was starting to lose the room. He bit his lip, then raised one finger in the air. "There's research, and then there's common sense. Anyone who has difficulty taking notes by hand—they can use a computer. Plenty of schools have students do that already."

"Some students can't do that," said Violet.

"What do you mean, they can't? Schools teach kids how to type."

"You're assuming all kids are the same. Isn't it possible some of them *have* to write things out by hand, for one reason or another? If you try some of that research you scorn, you might come across something called neuro-divergence."

"I don't sc—!" Pressler caught himself, but it was too late. He'd just fallen for the same type of trap he liked to set for others, and the wave of murmurs throughout the room signified that everyone else had caught it.

Violet didn't seem to be enjoying Pressler's discomfiture, but her eyes shone with quiet ferocity. Something about this was personal for her.

Pressler chewed his tongue. His blazing eyes and reddening cheeks said the kid gloves were coming off. "I take it *you're* good at writing in cursive. *You* use it to take notes." He pointed straight at her, arm outstretched.

Violet's calm demeanor was unstirred as she replied, "In my case, I don't take notes. But I think it might be beneficial for others—"

"You wanna tell that to all the kids who hated learning it?! Who *still* hate learning it?!"

A stunned silence fell over the room. Trisha had the feeling that no one here had ever seen Pressler lose his cool like this.

"If they hate learning anything," Violet pointed out mildly, "then, like I said, the problem might be not *what* they're learning, but *how* they're being taught."

"So now you're trying to blame the hard-working teachers!"

Violet gave him a strange look. "Says the man who complains about useless knowledge being forced on kids."

Tension rippled in Pressler's shoulders, made his jaw stiffen. He was struggling not to lose his temper completely, as Toombs had done. "My complaint," he said, biting each word, "was about the expectation that kids learn *everything*. No one can do that."

Some of his trademark charisma made a half-hearted return as he added, "Einstein once said, 'If you judge a fish by its ability to climb a tree, it'll spend its life thinking it's stupid.' Now, I believe I've gone over my time limit—"

"School shouldn't be about being judged. It should be about learning to love learning."

"Easy for you to say! The girl with a 'perfect memory.' Not everyone is so gifted!"

Violet took a moment to form her response. "Even if I couldn't remember all the laws of physics, I think it's still important that we all know there *are* laws. I don't think I ever learned music theory, and I doubt I'll ever need to—for myself. But I wouldn't mind learning it, if for no other reason than to…to better understand people who *do* use it. It's the same with a foreign language. It's not just for communication, it's to help us understand other cultures." She glanced about as she said this and happened to catch sight of Trisha interpreting for Althea.

Violet turned back to Pressler and said, "Though if you want to talk about practical application, it looks like Veil could stand to offer an ASL course so events like these could have a hired interpreter."

Trisha's eyes widened.

The girl sitting next to Violet gasped.

At first Violet didn't seem to understand the stir she'd just caused, but then she looked down at her hands and seemed to register what everyone else had just observed: *that she had signed the words she'd just spoken.* "Oh," she said softly.

If Trisha didn't know better, she'd believe that Violet wasn't aware, until that moment, that she was capable of sign.

Trisha let her hands relax as Violet turned once more to

Pressler and said—and signed, "You could be right, Mr. Pressler. You could be right and I could be wrong. But you're not prepared to prove it. Which makes me wonder if you even care whether you're right or wrong, whether there might really be people out there who need those 'useless' skills you'd be so quick to throw away." With that, she sat down.

The crowd waited to see how Pressler would respond. Seconds passed. Pressler remained staring at Violet, unblinking. Finally he brought the microphone back to his lips, but at that moment Rod Piper's booming voice cut him off: "That concludes today's debate. Thank you, ladies and gentlemen."

V

"It's a trailhead symbol. Or at least it was." Trisha traced the outline of the leaf with her fingertip. "My parents have an old photograph of me with my grandparents when I was little. I guess it was the last time I saw them. They took me camping on the Lammwych Hiking Trail. I don't really have any memories of them, so that photo is all I have to remember them by. That's how I recognize this symbol; it's behind us in the photo."

As she listened, Violet could still feel residual adrenaline pumping inside her from the debate. Exhilarating as it was, it had been nice to stop thinking, for a few minutes at least, about the serial killer stalking the town. Perhaps everyone who had seen the debate appreciated the brief distraction—besides Pressler, that is.

Several people had congratulated her on her way out of the debate, and perhaps even more would've done so if the sheriff hadn't taken her aside and told her they needed her at the station right away. She'd gone with Jen to the sheriff's office (Cy was back in the waiting room, sulking about being left out), and they were soon joined by Dubowski, Deputy Benno, and this young woman, a visitor to Veil from Maine, who had recognized the image from Violet's memory.

Trisha's fingers were still touching the leaf symbol. She had beautiful hands, Violet observed. During the debate, she'd noticed them when she caught sight of Trisha signing. Her skin was lovely to look at, and her hands moved gracefully as they signed. Maybe that's why it hadn't hit her straight away, that she was watching someone signing and she *understood* what they were saying.

One thing Trisha had said stuck in Violet's mind. "Wait, the *Lammwych* Trail?"

"Yeah."

"Does it have anything to do with a girl who went missing forty-two years ago?"

"Yes, Roberta Lammwych. The trail's named after her father. Some people say her spirit still haunts the forest, and one day she'll come back."

"Mm-hm. I know," Violet said shortly. Embarrassed, she added, "Your aunt told me."

"Oh? Which one?"

"The hearing one."

Trisha nodded, amused. "She's gotten more interested in local folklore the last few years. I hope she didn't talk your ear off."

Violet didn't answer. She recalled how Delphine, at the time, was convinced Violet *was* the spiritual reincarnation of Roberta Lammwych.

Jen was helping the sheriff navigate the Veil community website. "There, I thought so," he said, pointing at the computer screen. "I've been on the Lammwych Trail before. The symbol on the trailhead markers is a bird, not a leaf."

"Maybe the symbol's been changed," Jen suggested.

The sheriff shook his head. "It's been a bird since I was a boy. That's longer than Miss Sinclair has been alive."

45

"Well, maybe when they replaced all the trailhead markers, they missed a few," Benno hazarded.

Jen turned to Trisha and asked, "Do you remember where on the trail the photo was taken?"

Trisha wrinkled her nose. "V-vaguely? I couldn't point to it on a map, but if I were there again, I might recognize it."

Violet realized in an instant where things were headed, and her stomach did a nose-dive. She covered her mouth and tried to quell her rising panic with a deep breath.

Alarmed, Trisha asked, "Are you okay?"

"Miss Sinclair." The sheriff went to the door and opened it. "Would you excuse us a minute?"

Shooting one more look of concern toward Violet, Trisha left the room.

"How long is the trail?" the sheriff asked Jen.

Consulting the website, she said, "Twenty-four miles."

He nodded. "That's at least two days."

A whimper escaped Violet's throat despite her best efforts.

"Violet." Jen came to her and took her gently by the shoulders. "Come sit down."

Violet obeyed.

"Are you starting to remember?" asked Benno.

Jen shook her head. "That's not why she's scared."

Swallowing her anxiety, Violet said, "I have to go on the trail. If I find the spot where I saw this symbol, the rest of the memory might come back."

Keeping her hand on Violet's shoulder, Jen said to the sheriff, "Permission to go with her?"

"Granted. You'll want to start early tomorrow, as close to sunrise as possible." He glanced through the window at Trisha in the hallway. "I'll see if I can get Miss Sinclair to go, too."

As he left, Violet felt a tear running down her cheek. Frantically she brushed it away.

"Violet, trust me," Jen reassured her, "when the sun goes down, you're going to be so tired after all that hiking, you're just gonna go to sleep and not care about anything else until the morning."

Violet nodded, putting on a smile of bravado. "Right."

"Maybe I should come, too," Benno volunteered, "give you guys some extra backup. Though I'm not sure how Trish would feel about that, if she's going."

"Trish?" Jen echoed.

"She and I...used to be engaged."

Both and Jen and Violet gawked at him.

Sheriff Dubowski came back into the office. "She'll do it. Hopefully at least one of you will remember something."

"Sir," said Benno, "I was just saying, I could also—"

"No," the sheriff cut him off. "I need all the rest of my deputies here in Veil, for patrol duty. We're short-handed as it is."

"But, sir, if it'll help Violet feel safer—"

"Benno, it's okay," Violet assured him. "It's just a phobia. Being outside at night..." She trembled. "I don't think it would matter if there were two or even ten deputies there. But I'll get through it."

"Well, maybe you don't have to go at all. Trish could go, and if she finds the spot, she can just take a photo—"

"Benno." Dubowski shook his head with his eyes leveled in a cease-and-desist glare.

"But, sir, we shouldn't be forcing her, as a witness, to go through something traumatic—"

"It's more than that," Violet said in a loud voice, before the sheriff could reply. "It's not just about me being a witness. Think about it." In a lower voice she added, "I *have* to go."

Benno glanced at Jen, nonplussed. "I don't understand."

Violet looked at him. "I haven't left Veil since I woke up here. I haven't gone on any camping trail. The only way I could have a memory from there... The reason I'm having so much trouble remembering it clearly...is if it happened *before* my amnesia."

Jen, Benno, and the sheriff shared a collective shiver as the full implications of this statement hit them.

"If it really was the serial killer in that memory...then it's possible..." Violet ran her fingers over the scar on her temple. Her hand was shaking. "He's the one who did this to me. He's the reason I can't remember."

* * *

As Veil settled once again into an uneasy sleep, on the edge of town, Myrna Redpath sat in her living room, sharpening her knives. She liked the feel of the scrape against the metal, liked the shine of it once she was finished. When she heard a faint creak at the back of her house, she was comforted by the feel of the weapon in her hand.

At her desk at home, Kelly Upshaw also sat still, staring at her computer screen. She had articles she needed to finish, and she would—just as soon as she could stop replaying that conversation with Cyanne Grogan over and over in her head.

Out patrolling , Deputy Derrick, too, was having difficulty getting a Grogan out of his head, but it was Cyanne's mother, Jen. He knew he should be concentrating on his duty, but he felt compelled to address the question—why had he defended Jen Grogan to the sheriff?

Jen, under orders by the sheriff to get plenty of sleep before the next day's mission, lay awake in bed thinking about coincidences, and where Trisha Sinclair had mentioned she was attending college. These thoughts tended toward a particular direction, which brought her anxiety—but also, to her surprise, a sense of relief…

Thirty-five-year-old Chuck Benz knew he should be preparing for his big event two nights from now, but for hours he hadn't moved from the windowsill at the front of his house, his eyes glued to the activity outside. Two deputies were passing just now, shining flashlights between the houses on the far side of the street. How exciting it must be to be a deputy on patrol, Chuck thought. He wished he could be part of the action. Of course he'd tried to join the sheriff's department straight out of high school—but best not to dwell on that. Much more fun it was to imagine what would happen if he caught sight of someone out after curfew—someone suspicious, someone mysterious—and if he ventured out into the night to assist the deputies in chasing down and catching the shadowy figure. What a hero he'd be!

Rod Piper sat alone at his dining table with a single cup of cocoa, staring into empty space. He took a breath and spoke: "The sheriff's department has just announced that they have discovered the body of—no." He grimaced, inhaled through his nose, and tried again. "We have grave news to report today. The sheriff's department has discovered another victim of the serial killer terrorizing our village. I'm sad to report that the victim was…" He made a face. It still wasn't quite right.

All of them knew.

One of these nights, another of them was going to fall victim to the killer.

VI

Violet felt the bite of the wintry air on her ears. As she tugged on a hat, she looked up. The sky was overcast and grim. She thought she felt a raindrop on her cheek. "Is this really a good day to go camping?" she asked meekly.

"Oh, yeah," said Cy, grunting as she lugged her gear out of the car and hoisted it onto her back. "I've gone camping in way worse than this. One time my dad took me and Azura to this place up in Maine. The trail was so flooded, we had to climb trees and jump from branch to branch."

"Oh. Thanks." Violet tugged on her own pack and turned to regard the entrance to the trail, an opening in a line of trees just outside the village of Veil. Theirs was the only vehicle in the adjoining parking lot.

"What about Roswell?" she asked, suddenly thinking of the Grogans' calico cat. "Is he gonna be okay?"

"The Dosleys are taking care of him," Cy assured her.

"What do we do if it snows? Do we have anything to—"

"Hey, Violet." Jen appeared and patted her shoulder. "Last time we thought we'd be spending a night outdoors, we weren't prepared. This time we are. Plus, despite what Cy might tell you, I actually do know how to have fun, so between the three of us, we're gonna have a great time."

"Hey, make that four of us." Trisha stepped around from behind the car, pulling a headband down over her ears. "And if it does snow, it's gonna be beautiful."

Jen glanced into the car once more. "Everyone got their gear?" When everyone replied in the affirmative, she shut the door. She gestured for Trisha to lead the way into the forest.

They were nearing the threshold of the trail when they heard the noise of an engine. They turned to see another vehicle pull into the parking lot. This one was a luxury SUV; Violet had seen it before. It pulled up beside them and the driver alighted.

Jen stepped forward. "Something we can help you with, Mr. Pressler?"

Pressler didn't answer at first. His eyes flicked to one side to regard Violet, then to the other, toward Cy, who looked away from him. "I know what it is you're doing," he said.

"How could you know that?" Jen asked sharply.

Pressler made no reply.

"Well, it's very nice of you to see us off," said Jen, a harder edge in her voice, "but we've got to get started if we want to make good time."

Pressler pulled something out of his pocket. "I'd like to lend you this," he said woodenly.

Jen eyed the object in his hand dubiously. "That's very generous of you, but we have our own satellite phone."

"From the sheriff, yes, I know." He held the phone out farther. "I also know the budget your department operates on. Please. Take this one."

For a minute there was a battle of stares. Jen's discomfiture became more visible as she struggled with indecision. Finally the matter was resolved when Cy, without a word to either of them, cut in front of her mother, plucked the phone from

Pressler's hand, and forged ahead down the trail. The others followed, leaving Pressler staring after them from the trailhead.

"How *did* he know about us going on the trail today?" Violet whispered.

"That is a very good question," Jen replied, not a little vexed.

* * *

Over the course of the morning, Jen and Cy took it in turns to keep Violet engaged in a steady stream of conversation, so as to keep her mind off the dread of spending the night in the wilderness. They let the chatter ease off any time it seemed Violet was becoming too winded, but as the trail tended to be more level than steep, she seldom ran out of breath.

Trisha kept silent during the morning leg of the journey, and the others assumed she was focused on the hike. However, when they broke for lunch, Trisha hesitantly began to ask Violet about her amnesia. It seemed her aunts had told her all about Violet's adventures and she'd been too shy to broach the subject before.

As the afternoon leg brought them deep into a forest valley, and the ambient light dimmed to a premature twilight, Jen and Cy found their strategy no longer necessary, as Violet and Trisha were enmeshed in animated conversation.

"I actually felt a little guilty when you mentioned Veil having no ASL interpreter. No, I mean you were great!" Trisha added hastily when she saw Violet's rueful expression. "Everything you said, I loved it. It's just, I was supposed to become a resident ASL interpreter, back when Benno and I planned to move to Veil together." She looked a little bashful.

"Benno mentioned you and he had been engaged," said Violet, trying to save her from embarrassment.

Cy, who had been dying to hear this story since yesterday, quickened her pace and edged closer to Trisha, to listen.

"We'd both found jobs in the area. Benno had finished his training and was about to become a deputy, and I was set to teach elementary school, with some work as an interpreter on the side. My hope was that I'd eventually start offering ASL workshops for kids and adults."

"What changed your mind?" asked Violet.

"I haven't exactly changed my mind," said Trisha. "My goals are still the same. It's just…" She gave a weary sigh. "I've had to explain this to so many people—my family, Benno. Benno's being way more understanding than I deserve. My family thinks I'm putting off my career because I'm afraid, but that's not it at all. I can't wait to be a teacher. But there are different schools of thought when it comes to educational psychology and the best tools for teaching. Some of them even flatly contradict each other. Some say there's a lot about human behavior and learning that we'll never understand; others say there's a lot more we can learn right now if we let go of our preconceived ideas."

"You sound really passionate about it," said Violet.

"I am," said Trisha, frowning a little. "But I was passionate about building a life with Benno, too. I didn't leave him just to indulge a curiosity. I thought about it a lot and decided that to be the best teacher I could be, I had to—" Suddenly she yelped. As she'd been speaking, her attention had strayed from the path ahead of her, and her course had veered far enough to the side that her foot found a gnarled root. She pitched forward, but Violet snaked out a hand and caught her, saving her from a faceful of dirt.

Trisha wobbled as she righted herself. "Whoa. Thanks." She clung to the front of Violet's jacket, and the two of them found their faces inches apart.

"You okay?" asked Jen.

Trisha seemed not to hear her at first, her gaze lingering on Violet's eyes.

Violet began to blush, but she didn't pull away.

Finally Trisha blinked and let go of her. "Yeah, I'm fine."

"I think we should start looking for a place to make our campsite," Jen suggested. "We've got about an hour before dusk." She and Trisha marched on while the others hung back. Some of Violet's gear had fallen loose, and Cy helped her secure it.

"I think she likes you," Cy said in a low voice. When Violet didn't answer, she gently prodded, "Do you like her?"

"I just met her," Violet deflected.

"You and Candy were flirting with each other less than an hour after you'd met."

"Shut up."

"I mean, what, is it a pheromone thing or—"

"Shut *up*."

* * *

"This is Sheriff Dubowski."

"Sheriff, it's Grogan. We've made camp for the night. I'm pretty sure we covered almost ten miles."

"Anything to report?"

"No. Every trail marker we've seen so far is the new one, the one with the bird, not the leaf."

"Okay. Any sign of anyone else?"

"No, sir. Apparently we're the only ones hiking the trail."

"How's Violet holding up?"

"She's doing better than I think any of us expected, sir. I'm hoping we cured her phobia."

"Good to hear. Let me know the moment she starts to remember anything."

"Yes, sir… Sheriff, has anything happened in Veil?"

"Anything bad, you mean? No, not that we're aware of. We're about to go on patrol."

"Good luck, sir."

Jen slipped the satellite phone into her jacket pocket. The one Pressler had given them was still presumably in Cy's gear somewhere. So far, the one she'd brought from the sheriff's station was working just fine.

She returned to the campfire in time to hear Cy say, "The first week she came home with us, we tried, like, a hundred different languages, just in case she might understand any of them. We just never thought to try ASL."

Trisha laughed. "So what other languages did you understand?"

"She knew some German, some Italian, and a tiny bit of…was it Greek?"

"Greek and Swedish," Violet confirmed, blushing again, though in the firelight no one could see it.

"That's fascinating!" Trisha gushed. "Do you think maybe you came from Europe?"

Violet shrugged. "For all I know, I came from Mars."

Trisha appeared to take this seriously. "Do you know any constellations?"

Violet tilted her head back with interest. Clearly she hadn't thought to look before. The clouds had cleared up in patches, revealing broad strokes of velvety black dotted with twinkling pinpricks. After a moment, she lifted her arm. "Gemini," she said. "Orion." Her finger moved upward. "Taurus is right above it, but it's behind the clouds. And there's the north star, near the Big Dipper."

"Which one?" asked Cy.

"Right there." Jen pointed. "Polaris is the tail end of the Little Dipper."

"Polaris?" Violet seemed curious. "Is that the name of the star?" She looked back up at the sky, her eyes darting from one star to another. "I don't know any of the stars' names," she said wonderingly. "Just the constellations."

They might have speculated further on the implications of that, but their thoughts were interrupted when Cy asked, with concern in her voice, "Mom?"

The tears on Jen's cheeks sparkled in the firelight. She drew her finger across her cheek bemusedly, as if just now having become aware that she was crying. In spite of the tears, she smiled at Cy. "I used to do this when I was a girl. Sit back and name the stars. With, um…" She glanced at their amnesiac companion. "With my friend, Violet."

Violet sat up straighter. "You had a friend named Violet?" She looked over at Cy. "Is that why you gave me the name—?"

"No," said Cy, shaking her head. "I didn't know about her till after."

"Does this other Violet still live in Veil?"

"She might have," Jen said bittersweetly, "if she were still alive."

All three of them could see the grief in her eyes. "I'm sorry," said Violet.

"What happened to her?" asked Trisha.

At first Jen didn't answer. She rolled from a sitting position onto her knees and, leaning forward, deposited another log onto the fire, which had been burning low. The flames grew and brightened with a satisfied crackle.

She sat down again and took a deep breath. "I was eleven…"

VII

"I don't think this is a good idea," said eleven-year-old Magenta.

Sixteen-year-old Violet gave her a fond smile. In the few years they'd been friends, Magenta had shot up by several inches. It wouldn't be long before the willowy tween was the taller of them. Lately she'd been wearing a magenta-colored bow in her blond hair, much like the purple bow in Violet's raven-colored tresses. Between her friend's blue eyes, Violet's green ones, and the amount of time they spent together, more than once they'd been mistaken for sisters.

"That's why you're gonna live longer than I am," Violet told her friend cheerfully. "You've got more common sense."

Magenta cast an uncomfortable glance at the *"CON-DEMNED"* sign in front of what used to be a six-story apartment complex on the edge of town. The top floor now doubled as the roof, its ceiling a distant memory, its walls crumbling to dust. The rest of the building was a decrepit, dark grey monstrosity. The fire that had destroyed it had long since burned out, but the structure still gave off the feeling it was turning to ashes before one's eyes.

Magenta turned back to Violet and tried to look and sound as serious as she could. "This isn't lack of common sense. This is stupidity!"

Violet giggled. "You are so cute when you try to sound grown up."

"Violet, this isn't funny! If you go in there, I'll—I'll tell someone!"

That wiped the smile from Violet's face. "You'd do that?" She sounded amazed.

Magenta seemed horrified by what she'd said. However, planting her feet firmly between the older girl and the building, she stood her ground. "Yeah, I would! I'll tell the sheriff! I'll... I'll call your parents!"

Violet stared, dumbstruck.

Magenta's bottom lip trembled, and she sniffled. "I just don't want you to get hurt," she said, more softly.

The inner corners of Violet's eyebrows went up as she smiled adoringly. "Okay," she said, taking Magenta by the shoulders and turning her gently round. "Let me show you something." She pointed at the corner window on the third floor. "That, right there, is where Mr. Rideau lived with his three cats, the ones I used to play with." She looked somberly into Magenta's eyes. "He only has two cats now. And up there, on the fifth floor, across the hall from me and my parents, that was the Landrys. They had a new baby a few months ago." At Magenta's startled gasp, Violet hurried on, "The baby's fine, but they were worried he might've gotten permanent lung damage from the smoke inhalation."

Magenta sighed. "Okay, I get it. But do you really think the fire was set deliberately?"

Violet waved her hand downward in a lower-your-voice

58

gesture, and glanced all around. "I do," she said, "but I don't know why yet. As far as I can tell, no one profited from it or got insurance or anything like that. That's why nobody believes it was arson. But I think I know what to look for now, and if I find it, then I can prove I'm right."

"Is that why you're doing it? Just to prove you're right?"

"A little bit," Violet admitted. "But also for all the people who lived here. They lost their homes and they could've lost a lot more. They deserve justice."

"But you're not a cop," Magenta said pleadingly.

"Well, maybe someday I will be. Maybe I'll train to be a sheriff's deputy, like Keith Dubowski. How does 'Deputy Hall' sound?"

Magenta raised a quizzical eyebrow.

"No? Well, how about this: we can both be deputies, huh? We'll be partners. Come on, Deputies Hall and Grogan, what do you say?"

Magenta finally cracked a half-hearted smile.

"There it is. Okay, we'll start planning that when I'm done here. If I don't come back out in fifteen minutes, then you have my permission to call out the National Guard and—" She was cut off when Magenta threw her arms around her tightly. In the past, when she did this, Violet used to pretend to gasp for breath. Now that Magenta had grown, Violet didn't have to pretend anymore.

When Magenta released her, the girl shrugged and mumbled, "For luck."

"Oh. Well, we'd better do two, then," said Violet, and returned the hug, maneuvering so that she could breathe this time.

Magenta inhaled deeply through her nose. Violet's scent was pleasant and familiar, something akin to autumn.

Before she knew it, Violet was disappearing through the building's front door. The teen looked over her shoulder, and her freckled face broke out into a smile. She gave a quick wave.

Then she was gone.

* * *

Twenty minutes had passed. Magenta sat on the sidewalk beside the overgrown lawn in front of the condemned building, staring hard at the front doors, her frown deepening with every passing moment.

One of the bullies at her school, Amy Chester, had bragged recently about getting a cellular phone. She'd be able to make and receive calls from anywhere. Right at this moment, Magenta desperately wished she and Violet each had a cellular phone. Or walkie-talkies.

Where was she?!

Magenta heard a footstep close by. It was probably a grown-up, about to ask her what she was doing near the unsafe building. She tried to think of an excuse as she stood up and turned around—

No one was there. Strange. She was sure she'd heard someone walking toward her. She looked up and down the sidewalk. Had she imagined the sound? No, definitely not. But there was no one here, unless they were hiding in the tall grass.

Telling herself she was being silly, Magenta peered at the lawn, trying to see between the blades of grass, squinting...

"Yo!"

Magenta jumped and spun around, then heaved a sigh of relief to see Violet leaning out a fourth-story window in the building. "You scared me!" she chided her.

"Sorry," laughed Violet. "What were you looking at in the grass?"

"Nothing. Are you coming down?"

"In a second. I just wanted to check if I could see the streetlight from this room."

"Why?"

"Because I think—"

Magenta shrieked as something shot out of the grass a few feet away and streaked past her, its white cotton tail bobbing up and down with each bound.

She put a hand to her racing heart and laughed. "Oh my god, I've never been scared by a bunny before. Did you see that?" She turned back to the window.

Violet wasn't there.

"Violet? Hey, Violet!" Magenta took a few steps into the grass. "Violet!!" The window stayed empty. Or—was it *that* window, or another one further along? No, it was the first one, she was sure of it. Or was she?

Feeling a chill in her heart, Magenta fairly screamed, "Violet, come back!!!"

But Violet didn't reappear.

Magenta considered going for help. Then an image appeared in her mind: Violet, having fallen, trapped somewhere, too hurt to move or cry out—*alone.*

Magenta went into the building.

Although she wasn't sure exactly which room it had been, Magenta was certain she'd seen her friend on the fourth floor. All she had to do was get to that floor and check the rooms along the front of the building. Only one problem: the inside was a mess. As soon as she stepped through the front door, she found herself struggling to wade through the rubble, debris upsetting her footing. She blinked hard to make her eyes adjust to the dim light.

The first staircase she came to was blocked by a fallen piece of the wall, and some of the steps were missing. She plodded along till she found another staircase, but this one only went up two floors before she encountered a similar obstacle. Even when she reached the fourth story, most of the doors were barricaded by caved-in sections of the wall and—Magenta nearly discovered the hard way—gaping holes in the floor. Fortunately the cave-ins made it possible for her to navigate from one room to another, but when she made it to what she'd thought was the front side of the building, she found herself staring out at the back lawn.

Frantically she hollered, "Violet!! Where are you?!!"

She felt tears coming. Even if she found Violet, she wasn't sure she even knew her own way back through the labyrinth of broken beams and hills of plaster. And it might have been her imagination, but it seemed to be getting darker inside.

Magenta took a deep breath and tried to will her fear away. She turned back to the crack in the wall where she'd entered from the previous room. Scanning the wall, she found another crack and followed it into the hallway. There she nearly jumped as she thought she spotted another person, but relaxed as she saw it was only her reflection in a tall mirror.

She skirted another hole in the floor, through which she could see two floors down. Then she found a narrow crack in the wall close to the floor. She kicked at the splintering wooden planks until they gave way, and crawled through. Finally she found a door that wasn't obstructed, though by now she'd completely lost her sense of direction and had no idea if this was the direction she wanted to—

On the other side of the door lay the prone form of a young woman whose head was a bloody mess.

Magenta wanted to scream, but there was a lump in her throat. From the back, she could already tell who it was, though she fought hard not to believe it. Maybe it wasn't as bad as it looked. Underneath all the blood, maybe the wound was superficial.

She circled the body and knelt by her friend. Violet's neck was at an odd angle. Despite all the blood, Magenta would've tried to adjust the head so as to reduce her friend's discomfort, but she hesitated, for fear that touching Violet might hurt her worse than she already was. She settled for gently gripping the girl's shoulder.

In the smallest of voices she said, "Violet?"

Violet drew a shallow breath and her eyelids fluttered. Hope bloomed inside Magenta—Violet was alive! She was going to be okay!

Magenta brushed bloody locks of hair out of Violet's face. "Hey," she said breathlessly, "don't worry, I'm gonna take care of you. You'll be all right. What happened to you?"

Violet stared up at her blearily. She didn't seem to have heard her, or even realized that Magenta had spoken. Her hand lifted, faltered. Magenta gently grasped her hand and guided it to her face. Violet caressed her cheek. Her eyes crinkled and her mouth twitched with the ghost of a smile.

Then the light in her eyes darkened and her hand slid to the floor.

"No..."

The first sob felt ripped from Magenta's chest. She laid her head on Violet's still form, her body racking with sobs. An even bigger wave of horror and grief washed over her as she felt the absence of a heartbeat.

How did this happen? The question reverberated in Magenta's head, but at first she ignored it, not ready to accept that

Violet was no longer a part of her life. Then something stirred within her, an instinct, an alarm bell clanging, telling her she should be giving the question more attention.

Unwillingly Magenta lifted her head from Violet's body. Saw the blood all over her head…but nowhere else. There was no blood anywhere in the room except where the body lay. Whatever had struck Violet's head had been in this room, but it wasn't here anymore.

A chilling realization dawned on Magenta, and she staggered to her feet.

Retracing her path backward was impossible, though she tried anyway. She knew it would do no good to try to keep silent as she proceeded, so she tried to go faster, but all that did was make her get more lost. Down the hall, she spotted another young girl, and realized that if that was the mirror she'd passed earlier, then she was not at all where she'd thought she was, and she backtracked. She came across a familiar-looking staircase, but was it really the one she'd come up earlier? Apparently not—the bottom steps had caved in. She hopped over them with agility borne of terror.

It was just after she'd reached the second floor that she heard it: the soft creak of wood, the bending of a floorboard in one of the nearby rooms. True, the building was falling apart and so it could be any number of natural occurrences. But Magenta had a deep gut feeling. She knew…

I'm not alone.

She just had to find one more staircase. Once on the ground floor, if she couldn't find a door, she could break some glass and climb out a window.

She could see two staircases from her current position. Getting to one of them involved passing close to where she thought she'd heard another human being treading on the creaky floor. She made for the other staircase, lamenting that the direct route was blocked, though given the ruinous state of the walls, finding a circuitous route should be easy—

She entered the nearest apartment, turned to go into the next room, and stopped dead.

The adjoining room was likely a bedroom, but unlike any room Magenta had seen thus far, it was pitch dark inside. She wasn't sure if this was because the windows' blinds had somehow remained unmarred by the fire, or whether part of the ceiling had caved in, blocking the window, or some other reason. Whatever the case, not one object was visible beyond the threshold.

And yet something made Magenta's hair stand on end as she stared into the darkness. Her heart was pounding in her ears; she could barely hear her own breathing.

Except...there was something wrong with the sound. Magenta took a deep breath and held it.

She heard breathing still.

Magenta's legs shook beneath her. She was afraid that if she tried to take even a small step, she'd fall over.

Past the doorway she made out a wisp of movement. Someone was there, looking at her from within the darkness. Staring at her and not speaking. Someone who could see her, but knew she couldn't see them.

Part of Magenta really didn't want to know, but she couldn't think of anything else to say: "Wh-who...who are you?"

A sharp noise—metal clattering—exploded in the dark room and Magenta's legs gave way. She felt wood splinters tear at her palms as she thudded to the floor.

The noise continued, metal against wood, banging, but not

repeatedly, a sustained noise—*rolling*. Something metal was rolling across the floor.

The darkness spat forth a cylindrical object, about ten inches long, two inches thick. It was a piece of broken pipe. Magenta had seen such fragments all over the building. It barreled toward the fallen girl like a miniature steamroller. Gravity and friction slowed it, and it bumped into Magenta's sneakered foot, and stopped.

Magenta looked at her sneaker. It was smeared with red.

The pipe's end was covered with blood.

Magenta could never remember standing up. One moment, it seemed, she was staring in horror at the weapon that had taken her friend's life, and the next, she was charging blindly through the building, screaming harder than she'd ever screamed before. She dove through every doorway, every crack she could find, glancing back every other step. She couldn't see anymore, but she knew she was being stalked. Knew she'd never make it out of this building alive. Knew the awful thing would catch her and do to her what it had done to Violet.

In glancing back, she failed to see the hole in the floor in time, and she plunged into a different kind of darkness.

* * *

Trisha, Cy, and the amnesiac Violet all stared at Jen in numb silence.

The older woman's face shone in the flickering firelight. "I was found just outside the front door," she said woodenly. "Someone passing by saw me. I woke up in the hospital. I told everyone what had happened. They found Violet—not on the fourth floor, where she'd been killed, but on the ground floor. They didn't find the murder weapon. They concluded she'd fallen through one of the holes in the floor, to her death.

I snuck back into the building over and over to try and find the spot where I'd discovered her, so they could check for traces of her blood. But, no matter how many times I looked for it, I couldn't retrace my steps to that spot. I thought I could remember enough of my route to get back there, but it was as if everything in the building had moved around. Things weren't in the same places where I remembered them." She sighed and poked the fire with a stick. "It made the sheriff and everyone else think I was hysterical or trying to get attention."

"They never found out who killed her?" asked Violet.

Jen shook her head. "I used to think the murderer was following me, watching me. I drove your grandfather crazy," she added with a nod at Cy.

Cy scoffed in dismay. "No one believed you at all?"

"Well, one person did. One of my classmates. Probably because she tends to believe the worst about everything."

"Who was that?"

Jen smiled wryly. "Myrna."

Violet's eyebrows went up.

"Oh," said Cy.

"Who's Myrna?" asked Trisha.

"She's the one who wanted to bring a knife in to the debate yesterday," explained Violet.

"Was she weird back then, too?" Cy asked her mother.

Jen threw Cy a reproachful glance and opened her mouth to respond, but then she hesitated. "Yes," she said shortly. The others laughed softly.

"I'm sorry no one else believed you," said Violet.

"Yeah," agreed Cy, "that sucks. And if it helps, we believe you."

Jen's eyebrows went up slowly. "It does, actually," she said in a tone of mild surprise.

Cy sidled up next to her mother and put an arm around her, laying her head on her shoulder. Jen returned the gesture and planted a kiss on the top of Cy's head, her eyes shut in contentment.

The fire crackled on.

VIII

"Wait, wait, what does that mean—'hairs on?'"

"I have no idea."

"I thought you were the expert on this song!"

"The song, maybe. Buying pigs, no."

The sasquatch-like—albeit cleanshaven—Deputy Ziegler grunted as he and Deputy Benno strode along side by side. "Fair point. Okay, give it to me again."

Benno sighed and recited, "'If you want to buy a pig / Buy a pig with hairs on / Every hair a penny a pair / Pop! goes the weasel.'"

"Every hair…a penny…a pair…" Ziegler's blond eyebrows wrinkled in concentration beneath the rim of his wool cap.

Benno envied his partner's apparent inability to feel the cold as they patrolled the streets of Veil by night. Benno, himself, was shivering miserably. His annoyance at having to repeat the lines of the nursery rhyme was tempered only by the fact that it distracted him from the freezing temperatures.

"Yeah, no, I give up," said Ziegler with a shake of his head. "What comes next?"

"'A penny for a cotton ball,'" said Benno through chattering teeth, pausing to shine his flashlight into a darkened garage with the large door open. He saw no suspicious activity. "'A penny for a needle,'" he went on. "'That's the way the money goes / Pop! goes the weasel.'"

"Sounds like someone's getting a booster shot or something," Ziegler remarked.

Benno's shoulders were too hunched over to shrug. "I haven't come across any deaths by lethal injection," he said.

"Maybe it's symbolic."

"Symbolic for...what?"

"I dunno." Ziegler waved to a woman opening her front door to let in her dog. She seemed startled to see them, then relieved when she saw they were deputies.

"I don't think symbolism comes into it," said Benno. "It was literal pepper that was poured on Marcy's nose. If it was supposed to represent something—other than the fact that all these deaths are related—I can't see it."

"Hm. But what if the song itself is meant to tell us something? What if it's the key to why he's killing all these people?"

Benno glanced around but saw no one within earshot. "I don't know if we should be talking about it out here. The sheriff hasn't released the information about the song or the past killings to the public yet."

"Yeah, but if we figure out the pattern, we can predict the next murder, or the next victim, and stop it from happening."

"I don't know," Benno said doubtfully. "The details from the song are usually added after the fact. We couldn't have predicted or prevented Mulroy's, Foley's, or Marcy Temple's deaths based on the song."

"Hm." Ziegler sounded dissatisfied. "What was the line about the measles?"

Benno repeated his scan of the immediate area, then sang in a whisper, "My son and I, we went to the fair / We saw a lot of people / We spent a lot of money there / Pop! Goes the weasel / I got sick from all the sun / My boy, he got the measles / Still we had a lot of fun / Pop—'"

"Wait a minute, that's not right!"

"What?"

"That's not how it goes! The first line of that verse is, 'My son and I went to the fair,' not, 'My son and I, *we* went to the fair.'"

"Well, the rhythm was off, so I added a syllable."

Ziegler's voice rose to a pitch that felt incongruous with his tall, hulking frame. "You can't just *add* a word! Are you crazy? There might be a code or something embedded in the song!"

"A code," Benno repeated, deadpan.

"And we could miss it if we don't repeat it word for word!"

Benno waved with a tight-lipped smile to another passing deputy across the street who was too bundled up for him to recognize. "Rudy, if you've already memorized the whole song, why are you having me recite it for you?"

Ziegler clammed up with a sheepish look on his face. "It helps me think about it to hear it out loud."

Benno opened his mouth as if to reprove him further, then blinked and did an about-face. "Who was that?"

"Huh? Who?"

"That deputy we just saw. Who was it? No one else is supposed to be patrolling this neighborhood, just us."

Ziegler turned and peered in the direction Benno was staring, where the unidentified deputy had turned onto a side street and disappeared among the houses. "I didn't see them," he said.

Benno clicked on his radio. "Benno to all deputies. Please confirm if you passed by me on Mirror Street a moment ago. Over." He waited, but there was no reply. "I repeat, if a deputy passed me just now and I waved to you, please confirm."

71

"Benno, what are you doing?" asked Ziegler. "What's the big deal?"

"If you're trying to break curfew and do something you shouldn't," said Benno, "how do you get past the patrolling deputies?" When Ziegler didn't reply, Benno answered for him, "You disguise yourself as another deputy! I didn't even think of it till they were out of sight! That could've been the killer—"

"Benno, this is Deputy Derrick. I passed you a minute ago. Near the blue mailbox."

"This wasn't near a mailbox!"

"This is Deputy Hayden. Benno, that was me you just saw. I had to escort a girl home. She fell asleep at her boyfriend's and the jerk wouldn't let her stay over, even though it was after curfew. Tried to call in to report the deviation from my route, but my radio gave out on me for a minute."

Deflating with a mix of relief and disappointment, Benno responded, "Acknowledged. Thanks, Jess." He avoided looking Ziegler in the eye.

"The radios have been on the fritz this season," Ziegler remarked, taking pity on him. "Remember how Grogan's wouldn't work when she was out in the woods and her GPS was broken?"

They continued their patrol, and after a moment Ziegler added reflectively, "Maybe you're right. I could be reading too much into the song."

Thoughtfully, Benno replied, "Maybe that's what the killer wants. Maybe *that's* the point of the song—to distract us from another pattern in the killings."

Ziegler frowned. "But if it weren't for the song, we wouldn't even know the killings were connected in the first place."

As they continued their patrol, Benno mused, "I wonder

what would've happened if I hadn't caught that detail about the pepper. It was a lucky chance that I knew about it. Would he have just kept killing people, hoping someone would know the rhyme like I did? And what happens when he runs out of verses?"

This drew Ziegler up short. "Well, how many verses does he have left?"

"If I'm right about the past killings, just four."

"So he could kill four more people before he has to switch to a new song."

Benno shook his head. "Not necessarily. Remember, he got two victims out of the verse about the 'monkey on the table.'"

"Hm. Which verses has he not used at all?"

"As far as I can tell, that one about the pig, the one about sewing, the one with the grocery store, and the last verse."

Ziegler gave him a quick look. "I thought you said no one knows the order of the verses."

"The exact order, no. But in all the versions I've found, the last verse is always the same. 'Kiss me quick, I'm off, goodbye…'" He slowed to a stop, a pensive look on his face.

"Benno?"

Benno looked at him. "There might be one other verse the killer hasn't used yet."

"Which one?"

"The one I just recited, about the fair and the measles."

"But you said there was a double-killing somewhere, a father and son—"

"Right, but the song never specifies it's a *father* talking about his son. It could be a *mother*. Heck, if Violet's right, the killer could even choose a mother and daughter as victims, switching genders just like he did with Marcy."

A patrol car cruised by them. They glimpsed Deputy Derrick as he raised his hand in greeting. Benno wouldn't have minded getting to perform his patrol duty inside a nice, warm vehicle.

Ziegler's thoughts evidently ran in the same direction. "The sheriff has Tan parked in the grocery store parking lot. Is that because there's a verse that mentions the store?"

"I think she's more there to pull over anyone trying to drive into Veil this time of night," said Benno.

Ziegler was quiet for a long moment. The moment stretched into a minute. Benno started to hear the sound of his own teeth chattering, which the conversation had covered up.

"Okay," said Benno, breaking the silence. "You've got an idea that's bothering you. What is it?"

"Nah, it's nothing."

Benno deliberately waited five seconds before answering, "All right," in an offhanded manner.

Another five seconds passed before Ziegler gave in and said, "What if the killer meant for one of us to end up alone at the grocery store—because of the song?"

Benno seriously doubted it, but he told Ziegler he could check in with Deputy Tan. Ziegler activated his radio and did so.

By his third try, there was no answer.

Suddenly another voice issued from the radio. *"Deputy Tan, do you copy?"* Sheriff Dubowski rumbled. When there was still no response, Dubowski ordered, *"Ziegler, Benno, Derrick, rendezvous at Tan's position and report."*

Though running should've warmed Benno up, it only seemed to make him colder. He and Ziegler rounded the corner past the fire station and sprinted across the grocery store parking lot at the same time that Derrick drove in from the adjacent side. They could see Tan's patrol car parked in the far corner.

VIII

A new chill froze his bones as Benno spied a pair of legs lying on the ground, the rest of the body hidden from view.

"Debbie!!" Ziegler shot past Benno. He ran so fast he nearly overshot the car. Benno and Derrick caught up to him a moment later.

Debbie Tan's top half was completely underneath the front of the vehicle.

Ziegler breathed, "Debbie…?"

The legs moved. Tan wriggled out from under the car with something in her hand. She dubiously eyed the three men staring down at her. "Um, hello."

Ziegler was too overcome with relief to respond. As Benno helped her to her feet, Derrick demanded, "What were you doing under the car?!"

Tan lifted what was in her hand to show him. "Flashlight dropped and rolled underneath."

"Why didn't you just move the car?"

Tan thought for a few moments and then said, "Mm. So what are you all doing here?"

While Derrick used the radio in Tan's patrol car to report to the sheriff, Benno explained what had happened.

Apparently embarrassed, Deputy Ziegler exclaimed, somewhat abruptly, "You know what, I'm done trying to decode 'Pop Goes the Weasel.' It's just a bunch of stupid little unrelated stories that don't mean anything."

"That's because it's a metaphor for life."

Benno and Ziegler stared at Tan. "Say again?" said Benno.

"Life isn't just one story, it's a whole bunch of them, all disconnected. But they all still follow the same tune. That's what the song's about."

"That's deep," Ziegler commented, impressed.

75

Benno was more skeptical. "You really believe that?" he asked Tan.

She shrugged. "I thought it sounded good."

Derrick departed in his car without a word to the others. "Maybe I should stay with Deputy Tan," Ziegler suggested guilelessly.

Benno leveled a quizzical glare at his partner. Though he knew Ziegler's motivation had nothing to do with it, he had no intention of letting his partner escape the freezing weather while he still had to brave it.

"Dubowski wants as many deputies out patrolling as possible," said Tan, shaking her head. Then, after a moment's thought, she added, "Why don't I come with you on foot patrol? Benno can stay here."

Benno was saved from an ethical dilemma by Ziegler's prompt agreement. A minute later, Benno was warming up in the patrol car. Alone.

In solitude, he attempted to come to terms with the fact that finding what had appeared to be Tan's body had almost been something of a relief. All of them—not just the deputies but everyone in town—knew what was coming. The extra shifts and patrols were all well and good, but unless a miraculous breakthrough was made, sooner or later the serial killer would claim another victim. There was just no way to stop it.

Benno couldn't shake the feeling in his gut that he was missing something, and he was frantic to find it before the next body dropped. Most serial killers, he'd learned, were difficult to identify. They gleaned no profit by their crimes except, in theory, some pleasure or reinforcement from killing, so, without the personal element, there was nothing to connect them to the victims. But ever since Violet had pointed out that

Marcy didn't quite fit the pattern, that she didn't perfectly match the verse in the song that was the killer's signature, Benno had grown more and more sure that there *was* a personal element here. What could it be? A small town like this, the killer must have known his victims personally. It was, in all likelihood, someone *Benno* knew personally.

Wait—no—go back. He'd missed something. He could feel it. He retraced his thoughts.

Knew his victims personally... A small town like this... Knew his victims—

That was it. Victims—*plural.*

In Veil, the killer had claimed three victims so far. Everywhere else the killer had struck, there had only been one victim per town, with two exceptions. And on both of those occasions, each pair of victims had been dispatched—and discovered— at the same time. The killer had struck once, then moved on. Most likely, the killer had fled each town before the crime there was discovered.

But not here. Three murders over the course of a month? There was no doubt the killer was still here.

The killer had come home.

The killer had *wanted* to come home. Benno had no evidence for this, but he felt sure of it. Somehow the killer had a personal stake in this, but what?

What did Rob Mulroy, Matt Foley, and Marcy Temple have in common other than residing in Veil? Who could profit from killing *all* of them?

Was *that* the purpose of the nursery rhyme? The earlier killings, the ones that happened in all those other towns, perhaps *those* had been impersonal, by necessity, for some reason. What if the song was meant to spread the investigators' attention out among *all* the murders, rather than let them focus it too much on just these last three?

Benno shook his head. If there was something obvious connecting Veil's three victims, he was sure it would've been noticed by now. The only reason anyone knew the deaths were connected at all were the killer's own messages, bringing everything full circle, back to the nursery rhyme. Benno almost wished he'd never heard that stupid line about "pepper on his nose." If he hadn't pursued that line, then, at the very least, the killer wouldn't have left two corpses in his car for him to find—

"Deputy..."

Benno gave a start and banged his knee, twisting his head all around to see where the whisper had come from.

He saw no one.

"Deputy..."

He was here. The killer was here with him. By the grocery store.

Oh God.

Benno clicked on his radio. Static taunted him. He tried the car's radio. Same. Of course. The killer didn't want his victim calling for help.

He reached for the door handle—then realized the killer could be just outside, waiting to ambush him. Trying to ignore the throbbing pain in his knee, he pushed the buttons to adjust the side mirror. He couldn't see anyone lying in wait. Could the killer be on the vehicle's roof? No, impossible, Benno would've heard them climb up...wouldn't he?

This was stupid. Benno could just drive the car away from this spot, cowardly as it was.

But what if the killer were counting on him to do just that? What if there was a booby-trap—

"Deputy!"

Benno saw it in the rearview mirror, a flash of metal, clutched in a black-gloved hand—

He barreled out the door and went into a roll, then came up with his sidearm pointed straight at his assailant. "Freeze!!"

The figure behind the car gave a yelp and dropped face-first to the ground.

"Drop your weapon!!"

A six-inch cylinder rolled across the pavement.

"Identify yourself!"

The figure's earmuffed head lifted. "Uh, it's me!"

His brow creasing, Benno leaned over to better see the figure's face. *"Chuck??!"*

"Hey, Benno!" Chuck started to rise.

"Hang on! Stay there!" Benno lowered his sidearm and pointed with his other hand. "Chuck, what are you doing here?"

"Well, there's a prowler over there." Chuck awkwardly pointed behind him at a set of dumpsters.

"Why were you whispering to me?!"

"Um…because there's a prowler over there," he repeated. Somehow Chuck managed to shrug while still on his belly.

"Don't move." Grabbing a flashlight, Benno hastened to the dumpsters. It only took a few seconds to thoroughly check them over: no prowler.

"There's no one there," Benno told Chuck grumpily as he allowed him to stand.

"Aw, man," said Chuck, dusting himself off. "I followed him all the way from my house. I thought it might be the killer."

Benno doubted Chuck had tracked anything that wasn't imaginary, but he told him, "Chuck, you should've reported what you saw and let us handle it."

"Well, I figured you guys were all out on patrol, so I could just grab the first one of you I passed and—"

"Chuck. No. What you did was dangerous. Well-intentioned, but dangerous. And what is that?"

"Oh, this?" Picking up the silver cylinder, Chuck squeezed it. Benno nearly jumped out of his skin as, with a pop, the ends shot out three feet to either side. "It's an expandable bo staff! Cool, huh?"

Biting his tongue, Benno growled, "Chuck?"

"Yeah?"

"Go home."

"Yeah, okay. Hey, you should come to my retro movie screening tomorrow at the community center—"

"Chuck!!!"

"Yeah, yeah, going home."

Benno activated the radio to let dispatch know there'd be a civilian passing through Veil, then remembered it wasn't working.

"This is dispatch," said a clear voice over the radio.

Benno stared in incredulity, then gave a weary sigh and made his report.

IX

The Grogans had left Roswell, their calico cat, with full dishes of food and water, a clean litter box, and arrangements with their next-door neighbors to see to his needs the following day. They'd also left a few lights on around the large house to keep his spirits up while they were away. Now he lay, sphinxlike, on the banister at the bottom of the stairs, eyes on the front door, patiently waiting for his family to return.

A key jiggled in the lock. The cat's ears perked up in eagerness.

Elijah Pressler caught a glimpse of black, white, and orange fur shooting away into some dark corner as he shuffled inside. He just remembered to close the front door before he sank wearily onto the bottom steps of the staircase. He took deep, heaving breaths. He hadn't run like that in a long time, and certainly not in cold temperatures.

He'd figured, rightly, that he'd be able to sneak past all the deputies patrolling the area without difficulty. He was glad he'd brought along a radio jammer, so that no deputy could call for backup if they happened to spot him. What he hadn't counted on was that mishap on two legs, Chuck Benz, who had tailed Pressler for several blocks. If that rookie deputy hadn't waylaid

81

Chuck, Pressler would never have made it to the town line, let alone to the Grogans' house.

Feeling his limbs beginning to thaw, Pressler stood, pivoted, and marched up the stairs. Every spare moment since the debate, he'd directed all his energy toward learning Violet's true identity, discovering her real purpose here in Veil, and why she was determined to make life difficult for him. Maybe the sheriff's department hadn't had any luck identifying her, but they didn't have access to quite as many resources as Pressler. Which is why he was so frustrated now, having turned up nothing.

Violet's amnesia *must* be faked, Pressler had decided. The mystery surrounding her could only have been brought about by deliberate action. There was just no way a complete stranger with no personal history could simply pop out of thin air and become such a pain in his backside.

The first room he entered on the second floor he almost mistook for Violet's, so devoid it was of character. Only when he spotted the rows of deputy uniforms, short- and long-sleeved, did he realize this was Cyanne's mother's room. The next room he looked into was obviously Cyanne's, with all the photographs of her and her family (mostly her sister and father, he noted, but not many of her mother). He ducked out of the room as quickly as he had peeked in; he didn't want to invade Cyanne's privacy.

Finally, at the back corner of the house, he found the room he was looking for. With gloved hands he began methodically going through Violet's possessions—if they could be called that. Pressler noticed right away that some items in the room, such as her clothes, were arranged and organized neatly and meticulously, while others were strewn about and rumpled, such as the bed covers. *She's normally neat, but lately she's been distracted,* he mused.

Pressler made sure to check any potential hiding places for concealed secrets, feeling beneath all her clothes, behind her dresser, under the bed. Not until he lifted her pillow did this yield a result: he discovered a single sheet of paper, kept flat by a manila folder. On the page was a pencil sketch of a young woman, her face almost lifelike, her hair shaded to a strawberry blond. It took Pressler a minute to place where he'd seen the face before: it was Candace Windom, the local Wiccan activist. Her online presence had been practically nonexistent the last month or so, ever since that incident at her home, reported by the *Chronicle*.

Pressler looked around the room. No phones or computers. Whatever internet access she had, Violet would have to borrow devices from the Grogans. But he had a feeling this sketch had never left this room. Violet had drawn this completely from memory. Even if she were faking her amnesia, her powers of recall were definitely no hoax.

Beside the bed was a stack of library books on the subjects of Wicca and witchcraft. Apart from these, there weren't too many other personal items in the room. Pressler checked under the mattress, doubting as he did so that he would find anything—she wasn't a horny teenage boy, after all.

Beneath the mattress he found a calendar with pictures of scantily clad young women.

Pressler was thrown for a good minute. He experienced a spate of irrational thoughts—did Violet know he was coming? Did she place this here just to mock him? Was he on camera? For a moment he felt certain someone was watching him. He whipped around—

—and startled Roswell, who had crept up behind him. The cat streaked out the door and out of sight.

Heaving a frustrated sigh, Pressler turned the calendar over and discovered a Post-it note stuck to the front, with a short message: *Just in case your Candy crush doesn't work out. - Cy*, followed by a small drawing of a smiling, winking face.

Pressler looked around and felt a growing feeling of disgust. He'd come here, infiltrated the enemy's territory, to uncover his opponent's secrets, and all he'd unearthed was an adolescent crush. There had to be something else, some clue to who this girl really was. If it wasn't in this room, where would it be?

An unpleasant thought occurred to Pressler: What if Violet's amnesia were real after all?

Well, in that case, Pressler's goal was no different. If he found out her true identity, she'd go back to her old life, out of his hair. Everyone would win.

Pressler recalled a conversation with Cyanne at his Halloween party in which she'd mentioned that she and Violet were keeping a list of everything they learned about her, to use as clues to solve the mystery of her identity. Where would that list be? He hadn't found it here—but of course Violet wouldn't keep it, not when she had a perfect memory. It would have to be in Cyanne's room.

Pressler paused.

He stayed still long enough that the curious Roswell ventured back into the room to examine the intruder. Pressler looked into the cat's dilated eyes. Swallowing, he said, "All I'm going to look for is the list. I'm not going to pry into any of her private things." The cat continued to stare at him, the way it might stare at a bird or a squirrel. "They wouldn't just show it to me if I asked! I have to do it this way," Pressler insisted, as if the cat had made an accusation. "It's not going to hurt her if she doesn't know I was here. Besides, what if, in her old life, Violet has ties to the mob or something? Her being here could bring trouble. I could be saving Cyanne's life." With that, he carefully put everything in the room back as he'd found it, and went along to Cyanne's room.

His search here was conducted very differently from the previous room. He stood just inside the door, playing his eyes over every visible surface, reasoning—hoping—that the list was something she'd keep where she could easily grab it, anytime she or Violet made a discovery that should be recorded. Would the list be a single sheet of paper, or would it be in a notebook?

He caught sight of something on Cyanne's night stand. It was small, bound in faux leather, with a pen strapped to the spine.

A diary? Or the list?

Or both?

Pressler strode across the room. The object looked no less like a diary up close than it had from afar. He stared at it another minute before he reached for it.

The moment his fingertips brushed the cover, he drew his hand away. "You know," he said, turning to regard the cat who had followed him in, and subconsciously wiping his hand on his shirt, "she probably took the list with her on the camping trip. So this probably isn't it." Then he looked back at the diary, hesitating. "No," he said, as if convinced. But still he lingered. Tension flickered across his face. "No!" he barked, and he started to leave the room, sending the cat skittering out of the way.

Halfway to the door, his attention was arrested. His steps diverted and took him to Cyanne's desk. Evidently she had some homework left to do once she returned from the hike:

several textbooks and notebooks were heaped in apparent disarray. But what had riveted Pressler's attention was the writing on the notepaper.

It was in *cursive*.

All of it. Pages and pages and pages, all in scribbled, illegible cursive—illegible to him, that is. Naturally Cyanne had no trouble reading her own writing. But then, when they were her own notes, no one else needed to.

What was it Violet had said at the debate? *"Maybe you don't have any use for it, but couldn't there be people who do?"*

Cyanne's writing on the note on the calendar had been printed, but for schoolwork, she chose to use cursive. Small wonder, too, for if she tried to print such copious notes, it might take her so long that she'd fall behind. *But she doesn't have to use it,* Pressler thought to himself in a mental voice of protestation. *She could use a computer!* And he looked at Cyanne's computer.

It was a desktop computer, which surprised him—these days, didn't everyone have a laptop? But what struck him most was the keyboard. Each key had a bright red sticker with a capital letter, most of which did not match the letter already printed on the key. This keyboard had been programmed with a different layout.

Pressler knew there were some people who used keyboard layouts other than the normal qwerty. One of his former secretaries had immigrated to the US and knew only her own country's standard layout. Cyanne was apparently one of those who preferred an alternate arrangement of the keys, probably one that enabled the typist to type faster.

And yet she wrote her notes out by hand.

Again Violet's voice came back to haunt him: *"You're assuming all kids are the same. Isn't it possible some of them have to write things out by hand, for one reason or another?"* She hadn't been trying to make trouble for Pressler. She'd been speaking up on behalf of her friend. For some reason, which was none of his business, Cyanne could not type her notes. She had to write them down on paper.

And she'd been sitting just a few feet from him when he launched into a tirade against the very tools she used to keep up in school. How must that have made her feel?

He left the room in a daze, a cascade of thoughts overwhelming him. Not all of that tirade had been about winning the election, he told himself insistently. It wasn't all about his career. He'd had friends in school who were unfairly penalized for shoddy handwriting. Cursive had been forced upon students whose physiologies made any kind of handwriting difficult to begin with. But then, was that really evidence of cursive being a bad thing? Or was it evidence of flaws in education, just as Violet had said?

Violet. The palpably timid stranger who, for the sake of her friend, had argued for the unpopular side of the issue, knowing she'd have a whole roomful of people against her.

When was the last time *he'd* done something like that?

Pressler tried to quiet his mind as he descended the staircase, but the thoughts kept intruding. Could Toombs have been right about music theory as well? How many of Pressler's past decisions had been wrong? When had he stopped caring?

He paused a moment before the front door. This might be because he was reluctant to brace the cold on foot once again, or perhaps he wanted to convince himself that he wasn't fleeing.

He reached for the door, which was ajar, and pulled it open.

The other intruder in the house watched from the shadows as he departed and locked the door behind him.

X

Violet was amazed when she woke up in her sleeping bag and blinked against blue-gray light shining through the wall of the tent. She'd slept—soundly—the whole night through.

Her breath misted, so she reached over and pulled on her coat before she sat up and stretched. Jen's sleeping bag was empty. Violet could hear her outside, preparing breakfast. Cy was still fast asleep, her hair clouding her face. Trisha didn't have that problem, as her hair was short, though her face was turned away from Violet. Then she stirred and rolled over, nestling her cheek comfortably into her pillow.

Violet found herself staring, and she quickly looked away, uncomfortable. Then she took another look, her eyes drawn to that sweet face beneath dark curls. Even in her sleep, it almost seemed as if Trisha were smiling.

Trisha's eyelids fluttered and Violet was suddenly up and out of the tent, seizing her hat on the way out and offering to help Jen with breakfast.

The abrupt movement woke Cy, who grunted groggily. She and Trisha sat up and stretched at the same time.

"Good morning," Trisha said brightly.

Still half-asleep, Cy tried to yawn and ended up with hair in her mouth. Irritably she pawed it away from her face and tried again.

"You okay?" asked Trisha, amused.

Cy blinked rapidly but still seemed to be in a stupor. "I had a dream about you," she mumbled.

"Oh?"

"I was at your and Benno's wedding, and right in the middle of the vows, you and he got into a fight because you didn't want to take his last name."

Trisha seemed unsure how to react to this, but in the end she gave a chuckle that sounded only partially forced.

"Oh my god!" Cy sat up straight, fully awake and mortified. "Oh my god, I'm so sorry! I, I wasn't, I'm not awake yet, I don't know what I'm saying—"

"It's all right," Trisha assured her. "It's really not a forbidden subject."

"You sure?"

"To tell you the truth, he and I talked about me possibly taking his name, but we were worried it would confuse people since everyone calls him by his last name anyway."

"Huh. That's a good point. I've never even thought to ask him what his first name is."

"I don't think he minds," said Trisha.

As they dressed and rolled up their sleeping bags, Trisha asked Cy, "Just out of curiosity, what about *your* last name? Is that your mom's maiden name, or...?"

"Yeah, it's Mom's maiden name," Cy confirmed. "My sister, Azura—we have different fathers. She has his last name, and that caused Mom some problems after she and he divorced. So when she had me, even though she wasn't planning to leave Dad, he still let her name me Grogan. Otherwise, I would've been Cyanne Matutis." A somber look came over her. "I guess, now that he's gone, and since I don't have his name…he was the last Matutis."

In an apparent effort to cheer her up, Trisha said, "Actually I know a Matutis back in Maine, where I'm going to school. Charlie Matutis. He's this travel agent or something who used to live in my apartment building. Whenever he passed me or one of my neighbors in the hall, he'd always tell us about some great deal for going to Japan or Jamaica or some other place. I kept telling him I couldn't go, but it was still pretty sweet of him."

"Breakfast's ready!" came Jen's voice. Trisha bolted eagerly out of the tent.

Cy didn't come out for breakfast, even when her mother urged her to get a move on.

"I've been in touch with the station," Jen reported. "Apart from a few people breaking curfew, it was a quiet night."

"How are all the deputies getting enough sleep?" asked Violet.

"They're not," said Jen. "Sheriff's been trying to get some backup from nearby towns, give us some relief. Cy! Your breakfast's gonna get cold! Come on!"

Finally, Cy emerged from the tent.

Jen was immediately on her feet. "Cy, what's wrong?"

Violet looked up. Cy had a strange look on her face she had never seen before: troubled, and yet…no, she couldn't place it.

"No, I'm okay," said Cy in a small voice. "I just don't feel too good." Her hand hovered near her stomach.

"Do you need some hot water?" asked Trisha.

Violet expected Jen to go to her daughter and put a comforting arm around her, but Jen stayed by the campfire, eyeing Cy carefully and then saying, "What do you need, sweetie?"

"I'm just gonna rest for a little while longer," said Cy. To Trisha and Violet she added, "When you're done eating, why don't you guys go on ahead? Once I'm feeling better, Mom and I will pack up the tent and the rest of the gear and we'll catch up with you."

Violet was not at all sure splitting up was a good idea, but Jen promptly replied, "Sounds like a plan."

And so, after breakfast was over, Violet found herself hiking down the trail with her pretty companion, and realized she wasn't that averse to the plan after all.

Jen waited till the two young women had vanished from sight before she stepped back toward the tent. "Cy?"

Her daughter stepped out, showing not the slightest sign of illness. She looked her mother in the eye, her expression neutral.

"I know when you're feeling sick and when you're not," said Jen. "What's going on?"

"Mom," said Cy, "is Dad still alive?"

* * *

"So Cy and I pretended I'd seen the kidnapper, and that I'd just remembered who he was. And I pointed at him. And for a second, he and everybody else were just, like, confused, like deer in headlights, but then he took off, and Jen tackled him." Violet looked over to see Trisha beaming at her. Reddening, she turned away, though she continued to smile.

"You are amazing," Trisha proclaimed, stepping over a branch. "Sometimes you seem timid, but really you're a badass."

"I think a lot of it is that I'm just in the right place at the right time," Violet demurred.

"Well, not to minimalize what you've been through, but I wish I was more like you."

Violet turned to her in surprise. "Really?"

"Yeah! You and Cy and Jen, you bring about real change. My aunts told me all about what you've done since the three of you came to Veil. I've always wanted to be someone who changes things for the better—and I'm going to—but for the moment, I'm still stuck in school, waiting until I've learned enough. I keep telling myself I'm not procrastinating, but it's hard to believe that when I feel like I'm not *doing* anything."

It occurred to Violet that, were it not for Trisha, the leaf symbol would still be unidentified, and they wouldn't be on this trek to see where the trail of clues might lead next. If it did lead somewhere, if it revealed the serial killer's identity or anything that enabled them to prevent another murder, then it would be thanks, in large part, to Trisha. Violet opened her mouth to tell her so.

"You've got beautiful hands!"

Trisha stopped short. "What?"

Violet halted, too, suddenly wishing for a rock to burrow under. "I—sorry—that, that wasn't what I was about to say!" She struggled to realign her train of thought, to try to steer back to what she'd intended to...to...

Trisha was staring at her. Something in her eyes made Violet let go of her original intention and give in to the new impulse: "I just... When you said you hadn't caused any good changes, I thought of the first time I saw you, back at the debate. And that felt like a change. To me."

A blush started to creep into Trisha's cheeks as well.

"At the time, I didn't know who you were, but I remember thinking...that girl has beautiful hands."

Violet's heart was pounding, but not too loudly to drown out Trisha's soft reply, "Thank you."

And then her heart pounded harder—but much more comfortably—as Trisha stepped closer to Violet and gently took hold of her hand, lifting it before her face. "You do, too," she said, a moment before planting several small kisses on Violet's fingers.

Violet closed her eyes, lightly running her fingertips over Trisha's lips and cheek, drinking in the softness of her skin. She felt Trisha move closer, then felt her lips again, this time on her own cheek, then her own lips.

God, how she'd longed to feel this again…

* * *

"Yes." Jen's response was immediate. There was no hesitation.

Cy was so taken aback by this frank yet shocking admission that at first she couldn't speak. This may well have been Jen's intention, for she took advantage of her daughter's silence by saying, in a rush, "Cy, I'm always going to be there for you. No matter what, I'm not going anywhere—"

"Mom, Mom, shut up! What—what the—!" Cy started to sit, then rose again, she was so rattled.

Jen looked as if she wanted to dart in and hold her daughter tight, but she held her position, no doubt sensing it would provoke an adverse reaction. "Was it something Trisha said?" she asked. "I know Charlie was living near the college she goes to. I wondered if they'd crossed paths. I was hoping, for once, we'd avoid Murphy's Law."

Cy finally looked her mother in the eye, almost laughing in spite of herself. "He's been alive all this time. You've known where he is all along. But you just decided to tell me—"

"It was not an arbitrary decision, Cy." Jen's eyes were still concerned but her voice was hard. "Now that you've found out, I am prepared to tell you the truth if you'll listen, but—"

"I don't know, Mom!" Cy pranced toward her, thrusting her face toward Jen's. "I don't know if I want to hear the truth from you, because how do I know it *will* be?! How can I trust you now?!"

"Because I never wanted to lie to you. I did it because I had no choice."

"Why, did someone force you?" Cy asked sarcastically.

"Yes."

"Who?"

"Your father."

Cy guffawed in Jen's face. "That, that is hilarious, Mom. Dad, sure, *Dad* swore you to secrecy, to tell everyone he was dead, while really he went to work for some secret government agency to save the world from—"

"Not everyone."

"What?"

"Not everyone. I didn't tell everyone he was dead. Just you. Well, you and Azura, or else she'd have to lie to you, too."

"What do you mean, just me?"

"That's why I had us move to Veil. We had too many family friends back home who might give away—"

"Mom, what do you mean, just me?!"

Jen looked up at Cy, the ache and fatigue in her eyes more palpable than ever. "Cy, I'm sorry. This is going to be hard to hear." She drew a deep breath. "That last fight your father and I had…it didn't end with me kicking him out."

Cy scoffed. "What?"

"Though it should have," Jen muttered.

Cy shook her head, confused. "I don't understand. Why did he leave if you didn't—"

"Because he left us."

Cy was so stunned she didn't notice Jen moving closer, only registering after the fact that her mother was holding her gently by the arms. "He left us, honey," Jen said softly. "I'm sorry."

"No," Cy grunted. "That doesn't make sense. And besides, if he did, why wouldn't you just tell me?"

Jen closed her eyes for a moment. "The fight we had, that was him trying to convince me to disown you, like he'd done."

Cy's eyes bugged. "What?"

"When I said no, he wanted to file a restraining order against you. He knew he was abandoning you and it was wrong, and he was trying to make out like *he* was the victim."

Cy couldn't wrap her head around it. "But—but we were fine! Weren't we? Did I do something?"

"No, you didn't!" Jen caught Cy by the side of the head and held her, staring into her eyes. "You did nothing to justify his actions! I can't tell you exactly why he did what he did because I'm still struggling to understand it, myself, but *I know you aren't responsible.* He hurt you out of selfishness, and he wanted to hide from you confronting him, from accountability."

Cy began to feel sick for real. "Dad's hiding from me?"

"He said he was going to file the restraining order. I pleaded with him not to. It would show up on your record forever, it's completely undeserved. I offered him all sorts of things to make him reconsider…including telling you he was dead. I didn't think that would work, but—it did. With you not looking for him, he had no reason to, to…"

Cy's eyes were unfocused, her mind awhirl. Jen enfolded her in a tight embrace, which Cy did not return. Jen didn't seem to care. "I'm here for you, Cy," she told her again. "I'll always, always be here for you."

* * *

95

"I'm sorry."

"No, it's okay!"

Violet couldn't bring herself to look Trisha in the eye. She felt like a coward.

"Violet, it's okay," she heard Trisha insisting.

Taking a deep breath and bracing herself, Violet turned to face Trisha, who looked flustered but not unduly upset.

"It's okay," Trisha said again.

Violet felt she needed to explain. "I do like you," she said. "A lot."

"I like you, too." Trisha sighed. "But I'm gonna go out on a limb and say—there's someone else, isn't there?"

Relief tainted by shame poured over Violet. "Yeah. There is. I mean, I haven't seen her in a month, and she might not be coming back to Veil, and I actually haven't heard anything from her since she left, probably 'cause she's still working stuff out, and so she's pretty much unavailable—"

"But," Trisha broke in, "she still has your heart."

Violet heaved a deep sigh. "Yeah. Essentially."

"I get it. After Benno and I split up, it took me ages to acknowledge when I started to have feelings for other people. I felt so guilty even though I didn't need to. Sometimes you're in a place where you want to act on it, and sometimes you're not." She gave Violet a rueful smile. "Whoever she is, she's lucky."

"Thanks," Violet mumbled.

After a moment's awkward silence, Trisha asked, "Do you want to wait here for Cy and Jen to catch up?"

"Nah, I'd rather keep walking," said Violet, and they did so. Violet wondered what they might talk about next, and how awkward it would continue to be.

"So she hasn't contacted you at all since she left town?"

Apparently Trisha believed in facing awkwardness head-on.

"No, she hasn't. Though she did send Marcy to check on me."

"Marcy? Wait, wasn't she one of the people who—Violet? Are you all right?"

Violet had stopped dead, her eyes transfixed. Just over Trisha's shoulder she saw a trailhead marker, a sign with a symbol in the shape of a bird, like hundreds of others they'd seen since they started the hike. But in her head she could see a different marker—the one she'd seen before, the one with the symbol of a leaf. And she could hear the tune, the whistle, the serial killer's song...

The picture was there before her eyes, slowly taking shape. And there was someone in that picture, gradually coming into focus...

* * *

"This is Dubowski."

"Sheriff! It's Grogan! Violet's remembered!"

"What's she remembered?"

"Or she's started to remember, anyway—"

"Grogan, what does she remember?"

"When she heard...weasel...trailhead..."

"Grogan?"

"And she...saw Myrna Redpath in the...was whistling the tune."

"Grogan, please repeat, it sounded like you said Violet remembered Myrna Redpath whistling the tune, 'Pop Goes the Weasel.'"

"Myrna...trailhead marker..."

"Grogan? Grogan!"

* * *

Despite her limp, Myrna was in the habit of walking to and from the grocery store whenever she did her shopping. She was just exiting with a full canvas bag of groceries when two patrol cars pulled up to her. Deputy Derrick stepped out of one of them and said, "Myrna Redpath, we need you to come with us to the station for—"

Automatically Myrna whipped out a ten-inch knife, drawing gasps and cries from fellow shoppers nearby.

"Ms. Redpath, drop the knife!" Derrick commanded.

"You keep away from me!" Myrna screeched.

"Myrna, come on," pleaded Deputy Ziegler, who had just emerged from the other car. "Let's not go through this again."

Myrna kept the knife pointed in the deputies' direction. "I don't trust you!" she shrieked. "The only one I trust is Magenta! You hear me? Unless I see Magenta, you'll have to shoot me to make me cooperate!"

Derrick and Ziegler exchanged glances.

* * *

"Sheriff? Sheriff, can you hear me?" Jen jabbed at the buttons on the satellite phone to no avail. "Cy? Cy!" Her daughter sat, unresponsive, on a stump some distance away. "Cy, where's the other satellite phone? The one Pressler gave us? Cy!!"

In a corner of her mind, Violet felt concern for Cy, with whom something was clearly very wrong, she could tell. But her focus remained on the image in her memory, no longer elusive, just suddenly *there*, as if it always had been. "I see her," she said, eyes closed. "I see Myrna."

"And you're on the trail with her?" asked Trisha, standing next to her.

"No…no, she doesn't see me. It doesn't make sense! She's looking right at me! How can she not see me?!"

"Cy, you have to remember where you put it!"

"Wait a minute…" Violet tilted her head back, keeping her

eyes closed but letting them un-squeeze a little. In her mind, the memory was like a room in which she stood. She took a step back... "She's on a TV screen."

"What?!"

"Myrna—she's on a TV screen! I can see her, on the TV, standing on the trail in front of the marker with the leaf symbol."

"...just one of many natural treasures the incredible town of Veil has to offer," Myrna was saying, in a slight monotone.

"It's a commercial!" Violet exclaimed. "A local TV commercial by the chamber of commerce! I saw Myrna on a TV screen at the same time that I heard someone whistling 'Pop Goes the Weasel.'"

"Can you remember where you were, or when it happened?" asked Trisha.

Violet turned on the spot inside her memory-room. "Oh my god," she breathed. "It's Halloween. The community center— the Spooktacular. The chamber of commerce had a booth there, playing the commercial on a loop. I was talking to Marcy." As she spoke her name, she spotted Marcy sitting on the bench— alive, vibrant, comely. Sadness began to overwhelm Violet, and guilt, too—and she felt herself slipping from the memory.

She caught a fragment of a familiar tune, and she whipped around to locate its source. She zeroed in on a dark form making its way along the outer wall. She hurried toward it, but the closer she got, the more blurry it became.

"I can see the killer," Violet said out loud.

"Who is it?"

"I don't know, I didn't get a good look at him."

"Was he stalking Marcy?" said Jen's voice.

"No. He wasn't interested in me and Marcy. He was...he was heading..."

The blurry form stopped at a door at the back corner of the community center. A hand reached out and opened it...

"He went into a storage area behind the community center," said Violet, opening her eyes.

"Cy, we need that other—" Jen turned and found Cy wordlessly holding out the second satellite phone.

* * *

"The building manager will meet you there in a few minutes. He said that that room hasn't been unlocked since Halloween," Sheriff Dubowski told Benno over the radio as Benno approached the community center in his patrol car.

"Copy that," Benno acknowledged. As he alighted, he pondered what the killer might have been doing in the storage room that night. Using the party as a cover while he snuck into a room that was usually kept locked made enough sense, but what had he stolen from that room that he couldn't have procured anywhere else?

Benno rounded the corner of the building. Ahead he saw Chuck Benz unlocking the storage area. "Oh, hey, Benno!" said Chuck. "Just getting the video equipment ready for my screening tonight. Hope you're still coming!"

In a flash Benno understood. The killer hadn't taken anything *out* of the storage room. He'd put something *in* it.

"Chuck, don't open that door!!!"

"Huh?" Chuck opened the door.

Benno sprinted forward to tackle him.

A sound—similar to a 'pop,' but much louder—rent the air.

Epilogue

"It was guilt, I guess. That's why I couldn't remember. It was just a week after Candy had left town, and I felt bad for, well…being attracted to Marcy. Once I got over my guilt—once Trisha helped me—well, I didn't have a problem remembering anymore."

"Mm-hm." Cy didn't seem to be listening. Of course, she could've just been wiped out by the grueling pace they'd all kept up as they raced along the trail back to Veil, returning just before sundown, hardly stopping for food or rest. But Violet suspected something else was troubling Cy.

Before she could inquire what it was, Jen came out of the sheriff's office and approached them. "Benno's out of the hospital," she told them. "Trisha's gone home with him to take care of him."

"So he's not hurt that badly?" asked Cy.

"No. Just some burns and a sprained ankle. It would've been a lot worse for Chuck if Benno hadn't knocked him out of the way of the explosion."

"Thanks to your warning," said the sheriff, coming out of his office to join them. "You remembered just in time."

Violet made a wry face. "Wish I could've remembered sooner."

"Whoever set that booby trap knew that Chuck would be the next person to enter the storage room. This was planned long in advance. The town's been waiting, dreading the next murder, and you just prevented it. The town is in your debt." The sheriff clapped Violet on the shoulder.

Violet was spared from thinking of a reply as Jen said to the sheriff, "Ziegler mentioned a confrontation with Myrna. I hope you didn't take her into custody."

"We almost did," admitted the sheriff. "We had a dramatic face-off in front of the grocery store. Had to go down, myself, to try to resolve it. I tried to explain the misunderstanding, but Myrna was freaking out, so I let her go. She lives close enough that she could just limp home. Onlookers thought we were letting the killer go free. I had to send Derrick to guard her place from anyone who might try to harass her. She probably thinks we're keeping her under house arrest. I had Rod Piper give a report on the incident so that people will know not to bother her—hopefully." He gave a long sigh. "I've had enough for today. I'm gonna go check and see how Kurt and Amy are doing."

Jen followed the sheriff out of the building, with Cy and Violet trailing behind.

"Cy," said Violet, holding her back. "What's wrong?"

For a moment Cy was unresponsive, then she looked Violet in the eye. "My dad's alive."

Violet gave a little gasp.

"You knew, didn't you." There was no accusation in Cy's voice, but she did sound hurt.

"Y-yes," said Violet.

Cy stared at her a moment, then wordlessly continued toward the main door, where her mother had just exited.

"Cy, I'm sorry." Violet jogged after her. "I can't imagine what you're going through right now. I want to be there for you, support you. I…" She gently tugged on Cy's arm. The girl

102

stopped and gave her a tired look. She was drained, physically and emotionally.

"I promise, I'm here for you," Violet insisted. "So—are we good?"

Cy shrugged, and a tear rolled down her cheek. "I don't know, Violet," she said, and she went through the door.

* * *

"Dispatch…this is…oh Christ…"

"This is dispatch. Please repeat, over."

"This is Sheriff…Sheriff Dub… Oh God…"

"Sheriff? Sheriff Dubowski?"

Sheriff Dubowski stood in the center of Kurt Riner's living room. The room was in shambles. He stared down at the body lying on the floor, arms and legs outstretched.

Amy Chester stared back at him through sightless eyes, a large bloodstain over her heart.

Someone had wedged a huge hunk of cheese into her mouth.

* * *

The uncomfortable car ride home was driven from her thoughts the instant Violet entered her bedroom. *Someone's been here.* It was impossible for a person with a perfect memory not to perceive the total disarrangement of every object in the room. Whoever it was had tried to put everything back in its original position after they'd touched it or moved it, but each item was just slightly out of place from where it had been before. It was unsettling.

Violet had just turned to go and alert the Grogans when a sound halted her—a telephone ringing. It was a phone she'd never heard before. And it was coming from this room.

A cellular phone—a flip phone, of an older model—waited for her on the center of her pillow. It rang enticingly, though

103

Violet knew she should tell Jen, tell anyone, rather than answer it.

The first thing she heard when she brought the phone to her ear was the sound of someone whistling the first few notes of "Pop Goes the Weasel."

Then she heard...

"Hello. I hear you're going by 'Violet' these days."

TO BE CONTINUED...

WINTER IN VEIL

A Mystery Novella Series
by Miles Ledoux

Next time in Veil...

Violet's tears poured afresh as she sat across from the woman holding the notepad, who said gently, "It sounds like there wasn't anything you could've done to save that man. He was probably attacked before the killer even called you. At least you were there to give him some peace in his final moments."

Violet gave the woman a hard glare. "You know he wasn't the last."

About the Author

Miles Ledoux was born in upstate New York and started writing murder mysteries at the age of nine. His first paid writing gig was in 2007, when a local theatre chose one of his plays for their summer melodrama. He received other royalties after moving to Los Angeles for graduate school, where he wrote, directed, and produced several mystery dessert theatre plays. He also started a side business designing and running mystery party games while working as a martial arts instructor.

Currently the author resides in Springfield, Vermont. Despite having lived in five different states, he has remained active in community theatre as a playwright, director, and actor. He also has a YouTube channel where he compares Agatha Christie adaptations to the books they were based on. His handle is @MysteryMiles.

Miles loves books, cats, music, Star Trek, Peanuts, and owns an ever-growing number of variations of the board game Clue. His favorite author is Lloyd Alexander.

You can connect with me on:

🌐 https://www.ledouxmysteries.com

www.ingramcontent.com/pod-product-compliance
Lightning Source LLC
Chambersburg PA
CBHW071329130626
46556CB00004B/1810